Greta and Boris

A Daring Rescue

Greta and Boris

A Daring Rescue

Siân Norris

Illustrated by Robert Griggs

OUR STREET
BOOKS

Winchester, UK
Washington, USA

First published by Our Street Books, 2013
Our Street Books is an imprint of John Hunt Publishing Ltd., Laurel House, Station Approach,
Alresford, Hants, SO24 9JH, UK
office1@jhpbooks.net
www.johnhuntpublishing.com
www.ourstreet-books.com

For distributor details and how to order please visit the 'Ordering' section on our website.

Text copyright: Siân Norris 2012

ISBN: 978 1 78099 623 3

A CIP catalogue record for this book is available from the British Library.

Design: Stuart Davies

Printed and bound by CPI Group (UK) Ltd, Croydon, CR0 4YY

We operate a distinctive and ethical publishing philosophy in all
areas of our business, from our global network of authors to
production and worldwide distribution.

CONTENTS

For Bram, Kaelen, Evan, Oscar and Bella. I hope you grow up
to love books as much as I do. .

In which the night is fateful

The time of the night had arrived when all was silent in the Kingdom of Cats. In the little villages where the tabbies and mogs slept, everything was quiet. The only sounds were the soft breathing that made their furry chests rise and fall; and the curious hum of the trees and the plants. If you listened very carefully, you could hear the sound of the moon in the sky circling the earth; filling the dark night sky over the dark night land.

In many ways it was a shame that the whole population was asleep, as most believe the Kingdom of Cats was never as beautiful as when it was bathed in the silver light of the moon, reflected against the deep ocean blue of the clear and starry sky. The darkness gave it the air of mystery and aloofness so often associated with its inhabitants. The silver illuminated the dark forests and mossy banks, brightened the blue and red of the fruits and flowers, and made the lakes and rivers shimmer and glow. In fact, it turned the whole kingdom into the dusky grey blue color of the fur coat of their Prince, his Majesty Marmaduke Nikolai Boris Blue. He was the heir to the Kingdom and would eventually succeed his father, the King Marmaduke Nikolai Whiskers Blue, ruler of the Kingdom of Cats, Terror of Mice, Menace of Birds and Nemesis of Hounds, Surveyor of the Peace, Emperor of the Feline Race and Lord of the surrounding lands. It was a very fancy title, and although officially the correct way to address the King was as 'His Excellency and Most Magnificent Liege, His Royal Highness, the King!', his family generally called him 'Whiskers'.

The Blue family had a simple system of names. 'Marmaduke' was the name of the founding father of the family, followed by 'Nikolai', the name of the human whom Marmaduke was responsible for, followed by the name that the human gave each cat. In Whiskers' case, this was indeed Whiskers, whilst Boris had been named Boris by his human. The final part, 'Blue', was the equivalent of our human surname, and came from the fact that the current royal family was of that most graceful and beautiful breed, the Russian Blue.

The moonlight glowed over the sleeping kingdom. In the small villages where the working cats lived happily together all that could be heard was the sound of sleep. In the tall and imposing palace decorated with a shimmering rainbow of fish scales, the royal family and their courtiers slept. In China Town and Egypt Town where the aristocracy of cats resided in smart town houses or their country mansions, everyone was asleep. The kingdom was tranquil and peaceful.

But something was wrong. Over the soft noise of the night, the silent hum we hear without realizing it, another sound was reaching the ears of the plants and of the moon. The cats, deep in their slumber, didn't notice it; even the palace guards had succumbed to the heaviness of their eyelids. But the trees heard it, and rustled their leaves as they desperately tried to alert someone, anyone who might be awake. For the sound travelling across the land was not the kind and playful noises normally heard in the Kingdom of Cats. Rather, it was a fearful din.

Swish, swish, was the sound that broke into the stillness of the night. Swish, swish, accompanied with scampering and scratching of claws and paws, rushing forward through grass and fallen leaves towards the palace. And if anyone had been awake to hear it, they would have heard that each scurrying paw-step was landing in time, in the rhythm of a march. A soft thud, thud, swish, swish, echoed through the sleepy kingdom, as only the moon looked down on the onward journey of an army that didn't want to be seen.

The cats slept on, oblivious to the menace that was slowly surrounding them.

The pack of marching creatures started to head up the hill where the palace stood, imposing and magnificent. In the moonlight, the towering building looked even more beautiful and impressive. The rainbow-colored tiles glistened like tiny fairy lights, a blinding spectacle that illuminated the hills and villages below it. The army continued to advance. As the moonlight reflected off their furry backs, it became increasingly obvious which creatures of the animal kingdom were threatening the peaceful palace of the cats. And there could be no doubt at all, when one of the marching many kicked a stone and let loose a wild and pained 'SQUEAK!' before hastily being seen to and told off by the leader of the procession.

The moon could see the horrible truth below her now, yet from her lofty place in the sky was powerless to stop it. It was an army of rats. The rats had invaded the Kingdom of Cats. Under the cover of darkness, safe in the knowledge that every kitten, tom and queen would be sleeping soundly, they had made their cowardly advance, confident that no-one would be able to stop them.

The rats circled the palace, ensuring that in the highly unlikely event that any wandering cat should approach, they would be able to quickly and ruthlessly fend them off. The leader of the march, the General Melchior of the Rat Army, gathered around him ten of the biggest, strongest, most flea-bitten, war-worn rats who served under his command. The eleven entered the palace gates, stealthily, silently, and made their way up the stairs.

In which we meet Greta

The light streamed through the crack in the curtains to illuminate Greta's room. It was a fairly unusual room, but that was ok, because Greta was a fairly unusual girl. It ran in her family. Her father and mother were both highly eccentric, one worked as a museum curator and the other was a poet and writer. The room reflected the chosen careers of both her parents, as it was full of books, art prints, ornaments and artifacts; all from her father's abiding interest in ancient art and archaeology and her mother's interest in literature. But despite the influence of her parents' tastes on Greta's room, the feel of it was decidedly hers. The old-fashioned wooden furniture on which her possessions balanced; the wide window seat covered in cushions; the brightly patterned materials hanging from her sloping ceiling; the oversized Chinese dressing gown hanging from her door – it all worked in harmony alongside the piles of clothes, magazines, stereo and small TV of many young girls' rooms.

There was something very special about Greta's setting. She felt it to be entirely hers, the place where she always felt at home. Often, Greta felt it was the sole place where she could return to in order to be herself, where she was purely her own person.

Greta was a sweet girl. She had a happy outlook and loved to laugh. But she had a feeling that she never quite fitted in with the real world. She had lots of friends and did well at school – in fact she was one of the brightest students in her class – but something held her apart from the people around her. She often wandered off into her daydreams and fantasy worlds, preferring the life she lived in her head to the one she faced every day. One day she was an explorer, sailing the high seas and adventuring across jungles and deserts. The next she was an investigative journalist, travelling the world in search of the next big story. Other adventures saw her in the role of a dancing and singing film star from the Twenties, who led a mystery double life as a secret agent. In her imagination, every day brought new experiences and new promises. And Greta was sure that one day, these adventures would not just exist in her mind.

She was twelve, and although each day she went to school, studied hard and joined in half-heartedly with conversations over who was the cutest boy on TV, her mind was mainly flying elsewhere. Off into the world where she was a brave and daring hero of the French Revolution, fighting for freedom with the aid of a sympathetic, handsome peasant, a donkey and her white horse.

She was decidedly not in the world where her hair was never as glossy and her skirts never as short as the popular girls'. The girls who would giggle at her behind her back and laugh at her wavy bobbed hair or her clothes. Where the boys teased her for her brains and the teachers told her off for her dreamy attitude. At school Greta was happy with her friends, doing her work, walking to lessons, eating her lunch. But deep down, she was really flying away on the breeze of her imagination, and when she returned to her little and quirky room she could be fully content.

As the sun shone onto her bed, Greta yawned lazily and began to stretch. It was the first day of the summer holidays, and she had the whole house to herself. Her parents had gone on an expedition to Botswana, in order for her father to conduct research for the Museum on African Culture. Her mother had accompanied him to find inspiration for her latest novel, which she planned to set in ancient Africa. There had been much deliberation over what to do with Greta, but eventually the decision was reached that Greta's aunt would come and stay. Luckily for Greta, her Aunt Annie was rather absent-minded, and was happy to spend all day reading romantic novels in her room. She pretty much let Greta be, so she was free to make her own adventures.

Greta was not like some children who hated being on her own. She was rather a solitary girl, and lapped up the opportunity to spend the six weeks alone in her big rambling house. And with her cat to keep her company, she didn't mind the fact that Aunt Annie was barely around.

Slowly she opened her eyes and took in the brightness of her bedroom. She yawned again, and reached down to the side of her bed for her book. Now was the time to be lazy, she thought, lying back with the book in her hands until she felt suitably ready to get out of bed.

Oh! But it was so gorgeous to lie back on her rumpled sheets and enjoy the steady sunlight and know that she had nowhere to go, no-one to see, no school, no annoying people, no parents for over a month! No more having to rush around on the cue of the alarm clock. It would be a summer of long and lazy mornings in bed with a book and wherever she wanted to be in her head, followed by lazy afternoons in the garden.

After enjoying this warm freedom for long enough, Greta decided it was, at last, time to get out of her bed. She sat up and swung her legs round, slid her feet into her slippers and pulled her Chinese dressing gown around her body. She stood up and gave herself a quick inspection in the mirror. It was a beautifully ornate Victorian one that her mum had picked up at some antique sale. Greta grimaced, she didn't think her reflection justified the prettiness of the frame.

She was wrong of course. Greta had a quirky and intelligent face. She had high and distinct cheekbones, and bright green-grey eyes. Her hair was thick and dark brown, cut in a bob with a natural wave. However, when Greta looked in the mirror she saw an irregular face that wasn't as beautiful as the popular girls in her class. In short, Greta was an undiscovered beauty and would always remain so until she discovered for herself that it is inner beauty that shines through in the face that counts.

Standing up, she surveyed her domain in the dappled sunlight. 'Boris,' she called out gently. 'Come on lazy, it's time to get up.'

Normally at the sound of Greta's voice, Boris the cat would jump up from his bed and onto hers, nuzzling his human with a good morning hug. Yet Greta received no response. She looked thoughtful for a moment, and then decided that maybe Boris had stayed out, or was already awake. Still, it was most unlike him to not be in his normal place. After a pause to think, Greta reasoned that she had stayed asleep later than normal, so Boris was probably already up and about, seeing to the house and his duties.

She opened the door to her bedroom and stepped out onto the wide hallway. Greta adored her house. It was an old and homely cottage, full of nooks and crannies, staircases and big rooms with low ceilings and wooden floors. She wandered down the stairs to the kitchen, put on the kettle and put some toast in the toaster, before pouring out some milk and spooning out some chicken bits for Boris. She smeared some honey on her toast and finished making her tea, and then walked out into the garden. 'Boris wasn't in the kitchen either,' she thought. 'I wonder if he's sunbathing outside.'

Like the house, the garden was large and rambling, roses growing here, vegetables growing there. In the middle was a big apple tree that blossomed in the summer and gave fruit in the autumn, as well as providing welcome relief from the mid-morning sun with its shady boughs. She flopped herself down under its branches with her honeyed toast, tea and book, and once more called out Boris' name. But the familiar 'pad-pad' across the yard was absent, as was his inquisitive miaow, the push of his wet nose against her arm or book, his demand for more milk.

Greta and Boris had been best friends since the day that Boris had chosen Greta and come to live with her. It was impossible not to fall in love with Boris on sight. Like all Russian Blue cats, his coat was an exquisite smoky grey, whilst his eyes glowed amber and gold. He was rather aloof with everyone except Greta who he adored, and did his best to look after her as befitted his duty (contrary to popular belief, humans don't own their cats – the cats are assigned to look after the humans. It was Boris' duty to look after Greta). Meanwhile, Greta took him straight to her heart. She recognized the highborn nature of his manner, but knew he would always be loyal. To Boris she told all her dreams and fantasies, the adventures of her daydreams, her hopes and wishes. Sometimes, when the world got too much, she would dry her crying eyes in his fur; other days when the sun shone they played together for hours, and he would tickle her face with his long and regal whiskers. They were inseparable.

She tried to put any worry out of her mind. Like herself, Boris was an independent soul, and even though it was unusual for him not to accompany her in the mornings, she recognized that Boris had a busy life. He knew, she reasoned, that she was practically alone in the house now (Aunt Annie, after all, was a trifle absent-minded), so he was probably checking things out, making sure everything was in order and safe so that she didn't feel frightened in the old and near-empty house.

It came to teatime, and Greta dragged herself away from the now cooling garden. Picking up her books and cups and the flowing folds of her skirt, she wandered dreamily into the house. 'Boris?' she called out. 'Don't you want your dinner?' But still there was no reply. 'Where is that cat?'

She laid out some cat food in Boris' bowl, in the hope it would tempt him over. But there was still no sight or sound of him. She and Aunt Annie ate their meal, but Boris still didn't come downstairs.

Leaving the kitchen, Greta strolled lazily into the large but cluttered living room, crowded as it was with collections from her father's travels, her mother's own titles and the other thrilling and fascinating books she had accumulated over the years. She turned on the TV and curled up in her favorite armchair. But when she put out her hand to rest on where Boris' softly breathing stomach would normally be, he still wasn't there.

Having been calm all day, Greta was now beginning to get frightened. Life could be a bit scary without Boris. And she just couldn't think what had happened to him! It was so unlike him to leave her alone for this amount of time. He was a creature of routine, and to break it like this was out of character.

She felt a bit sleepy, and with a quick last look around the house for Boris, she returned to her bedroom, pulled back her eiderdown and even without him there to watch over her, she fell back to sleep.

In which the cats wake up

The moon had ended her futile vigil over the night sky, seeing but unable to do anything to prevent the fearful invasion that had happened beneath her eyes. She waved goodbye to the earth beneath her, and in her place the sun rose, mighty and bright. As his rays penetrated through the fading night gloom, the cats sleeping in the kingdom stretched their floppy limbs and opened their yellow-green eyes. The adult cats started cooking mice or kippers and heating the milk, as the kittens yawned and scampered around; whilst in the royal palace the cooks and chefs were frantically preparing the breakfast banquet.

Every Saturday, the King Whiskers (whose rather grander full name was King Marmaduke Nikolai Whiskers Blue) would invite the aristocracy of the Kingdom to the palace to partake in a breakfast feast. This meant that as well as the King, Queen Alexandria, (a beautiful and elegant cat whose full name is Isis Ashanti Alexandria Blue), Prince Boris, the Royal Princesses Aurora and Griselda and the young Prince Sweep; the chefs also had to prepare for the Egyptian family, the Chinese family, the French family, the Ginger Royals and Baron Silver, his six kittens and the Baroness.

The kitchens were frantic, preparing hot and cold milk, a selection of fried mice and delicately poached salmon, fried kippers, several plates of biscuits, bird wings, and a number of extra specially ordered items, manufactured cat food being a particular (although disapproved) favorite of the young Prince Sweep (full name, of course, Marmaduke Nikolai Sweep Blue).

Hot and flustered, but proud of his handiwork, the head chef of the palace (a white cat with pink eyes called Gordon) handed the platters over to the black-and-white waiting servants who would deliver the food to the royal banquet. At one end of the table sat the King Whiskers and opposite him sat the Queen

Alexandria. Seated on either side of her were the Princesses, followed by the guests, whilst on the left of the King sat Prince Sweep. But at the right hand seat of the King, Boris' place at the royal table was empty.

'Welcome my friends and kin,' purred the deep and rich voice of the King, 'to this great breakfast, prepared by the finest cooks in my vast feline kingdom. As ever, my wife and I are honored to invite your company to our humble table. I welcome my wife's family, the worthy cats of Egypt, and the great muses of China. I welcome my dear countrymen, the Gingers and Baron Silver. Friends and allies we have been for many years. And last but by no means least, bonjour! To the French cats, for whom there is always room at this banqueting table. If we are all here, then let us begin!'

'My dear,' said the graceful Queen in her deep and smooth voice. 'I am sure our guests were warmed and welcomed by your kind speech. However, it is impossible for us to begin this meal, as I fear we are not all present. You may notice the seat on your right lacks an inhabitant. Our good son, the noble Prince Boris, is remarkably absent.' (Do not be alarmed by the manner of speech employed by the Royal family. They feel a strange need to speak in long elaborate sentences, where a few words would suit just as well.)

'Good gracious, my love, you are right! Well, this is an unexpected delay. I had high hopes of this being a flawless and enjoyable morning in the company of our kith and kin. Now, where could the little scamp be? I propose we leave the table, and go and wake the lazy Prince up.'

And with that, King Marmaduke Nikolai Whiskers Blue stood to his full height, clapped his forepaws together, and the party rose to follow him. They trooped out of the banqueting hall, through the throne room, past the King's study and the now little-used nursery, around the regal fountain, past the gallery where the many portraits of the Royals and their predecessors were displayed, up the curving staircase which led to the Imperial bedroom, down the straight staircase which led to the hallway where the Princesses had their bedrooms, and up another twisting stone staircase, past Sweep's room and tutor's office, along and along, past the vista that looks onto the Royal gardens, until they finally reached the chambers of the Royal Prince.

'Now now, son, we'll have no more of this nonsense!' cried out King Whiskers. 'You have slept long enough and delayed the banquet. Wake up and join us for the feast carefully prepared for us by our good and generous staff below.'

Yet there was no reply. 'My dear,' said the Queen. 'Perhaps we should just go inside.'

The King opened the heavy door that separated Boris' room from the hallway. It was a simple room, a few books, a writing desk, a large comfortable bed and a picture of his human on the wall. However, aside from these few possessions, the room was empty. Boris was nowhere to be seen. The Princesses and young Sweep started to laugh. 'Boris!' they called. 'Come out and play! Where are you hiding? We're seeking!'

'Hush there,' said the Queen. 'I do not think, my dears, that Boris is playing a game.'

The King strode nervously across the room towards the bed. 'No my love,' he said, his voice graver and more serious than it had been for many, many years. 'Boris is not playing a game. This is no game at all.'

He bent over the bed and, lifting something from it, he turned to face his uneasy audience. There were shining tears in the King's kind eyes, and in his hand was the seal of the Rat King. 'This is no game at all. I am sorry,' he paused to repress a sob, 'I am sorry and regretful to have to announce, that Prince Marmaduke Nikolai Boris Blue, heir to my throne, future ruler of the Kingdom of Cats and guardian of its citizens, has been stolen from us by our mortal foe, that most dangerous of enemies, feared by cats, dogs and our human responsibility, the Rat King.'

A cry of horror echoed around the room, as Queen Alexandria fell in a faint to the floor. The Princesses began to whimper, whilst Sweep merely looked confused. The King let out a great howling MMIIIAAOOOW! of dismay. Quickly regaining his royal self-control, he lifted his head to face his blue-blooded subjects.

'The Prince must be rescued,' said the King. 'An announcement must be made.' He looked at his waiting courtiers with sad and solemn eyes. 'I shall meet you in the throne room but first, first I would like to be alone with my family.' Overcome with emotion, he bent to lift his wife to her feet, and gathered his three remaining children around him, as the weeping cat citizens bowed low and left Boris' room.

In which Greta's worries are increased

Greta was woken up on the second day of the summer holidays by weather that was far less friendly than the previous morning's glorious sunshine. Instead, the rain hammered down hard on the windows, and the wind fought and battled with the apple tree that less than twenty-four hours previously had provided such welcome relief from the hot rays of the sun. Greta shuddered and pulled her blankets up around her, for although strictly speaking it wasn't cold, the weather gave one the feeling that such comfort was needed. She leaned over to inspect her clock, and groaned when she saw its face. It was only eight o'clock! And she had decided to spend the holidays having long sleepy lie-ins, as opposed to early mornings of schooldays. There was no real fun in waking up early, unless of course it was to pursue travels and adventures. She lay back on her sheets and called out to Boris. There was no way he would be up and about earlier than her on this occasion.

'Boris!' she whispered. 'Boris? Wake up! It's time to wake up.'

She held her hand out of the bed and twiddled her fingers in a beckoning gesture. But there was no reply. For the second time that morning a shudder went through her. Something was definitely wrong. Boris would never, ever leave her for this long by herself. She knew him well enough to be sure of that. Her and Boris, well, they were only really ever apart when Greta was at school, or on holiday, in which case he stayed with Aunt Annie. This was just too different to how he normally behaved.

Greta all of a sudden felt a ridiculous desire to cry. It hit her rather too hard how alone she was in her house. Still, she wasn't going to cry. Not Greta. She took a deep breath, squared her shoulders, grabbed her dressing gown, and got out of bed.

'If he isn't in here,' she reasoned, 'then it's perfectly plausible that he is elsewhere in the house. Now, there'll be no more of this silly cowardliness.' Pulling her dressing gown tighter around her, she left her room and went downstairs into the kitchen.

After putting the kettle on and her toast in the toaster, she automatically bent down to give Boris his breakfast. But the plate of chicken she had left him yesterday was untouched, as was the milk that was beginning to curdle. 'Oh Boris!' she thought. 'What am I going to do?'

She spread the honey on her toast and nibbled it distractedly, wandering around the house to see if Boris was in any hiding place. Not that he was, or would be. So she found herself back in the kitchen and, for comfort, put some more toast on.

It was when she was sitting back at the table, toast in hand and tears being pushed back, that she heard scratching on the door and loud miaowing. She jumped up.

'Boris!' Greta cried, and ran over to the door to let in her drenched cat. Only, when she opened the door, it wasn't Boris sitting there. Instead, she found a small female white cat, with upturned green eyes and tan and black patches over her slim body.

'Miaow!'

Quelling her distress that it wasn't her beloved Boris, the cat-loving side of Greta's nature took over. 'Oh you poor thing!' she said, scooping up the soaking wet cat into a towel, bringing her inside and pouring her some milk. 'You poor little thing, you must be drenched'.

'Oh, well, I'm ok,' the cat replied.

Greta stood stock-still. She thought that the cat had just spoken to her, but she knew that was impossible, and that the only people who thought that cats, or any animals for that matter, could speak, well, they were a bit odd. And she may be a little unusual, but odd she was not. Even so, just to be sure, she thought she had better not respond. For the only people stranger than people who thought that cats could talk, were those who spoke back.

The talking cat let out a strange laughing meow. 'Aow hee hee. Don't worry Miss Greta! I know what you're thinking, and I promise you that you aren't going mad, it's just that normally we cats prefer not to converse with humans in their own tongue. It would be like you speaking French when you didn't have to. But when the occasion arises...' and she shrugged to finish her meaning.

Greta still didn't respond, and began to surreptitiously pinch herself to check that she was, in fact, awake. She was, and that didn't solve her confusion one bit.

The cat stopped her laughing. 'Look,' she said, her tone serious. 'If you are going to refuse to believe your own ears and eyes, your own sense in fact, we are going to have serious difficulties. So would you please just trust me on the fact that I am speaking to you, and would you be courteous enough to reply? I don't want to have to get high-handed and angry, but...'

Swallowing deeply, Greta decided to take the plunge. After all, no-one was here to see her talking to a cat, and she would talk to Boris without batting an eyelid. But as far as she knew, Boris had never spoken back.

'Umm, ok,' she said. 'I'm Greta.'

The cat rolled her eyes. 'I know who you are. That's why I'm here! However, I believe that I remain a stranger to you, therefore I will introduce myself. I am Miu Sumire Kyrie Mi-ke, a Japanese mi-ke cat, and I have been sent by my Lord and Master, His Excellency and most Magnificent Liege, his Royal Highness, the King Marmaduke Nikolai Whiskers Blue, King of the Cats and the Kingdom of Cats.'

'B...b...but why?'

Kyrie looked up at her, with confusion in her eyes. 'Why? Why do you think? It's about Boris!'

Greta's hands flew to her face, and she let out a little cry of relief. 'You know where Boris is? Oh thank goodness for that! Where is he? I've been so worried.'

'My dear Miss Greta, you are not the only one who has been worried. The whole Kingdom has been in uproar since the disappearance of Prince Boris...'

'Wait,' Greta interrupted. 'What do you mean, Prince Boris?'

Kyrie shook her whiskers. 'Boris is the Prince and Heir apparent to the Kingdom of Cats. He is the son of the King. You, Miss Greta, are not aware of the exalted role you play in our society. That the Prince chose you for his human is an honor indeed. But it is an honor that comes with responsibility. For it rests with you to be the one to rescue Boris and bring him back to the kingdom. The Prince has been kidnapped by our most mortal enemy, the Rat King, and you, as the Prince's human, have been chosen to rescue him.'

Greta sat heavily down on her chair, bringing her level with Kyrie who sat upright on the tabletop. All of a sudden she felt horribly tired. Everything had ceased to make sense. All she wanted to do was go back to bed and begin the day again.

'I don't understand. First you say Boris is a Prince, then that there is a Kingdom of Cats, and a Rat King, and he has taken Boris. And you want me to rescue him. I don't understand any of this. How can I be the one to rescue him, if all of this makes no sense to me? I didn't know any of this stuff existed until ten seconds ago. I'm sorry Kyrie, but you must have made some mistake. I can't rescue Boris. I'm sorry.'

Once more Kyrie shook her whiskers.

'Miss Greta,' she said. 'I cannot force you to rescue our Prince. And yes, I can see how this may all be rather overwhelming. But you have to help us. You are the only one who can help us. Without you to bring back Boris, then the fate of the Kingdom, of our homes, of our families – all of this is under threat. And on behalf of the King, I beg of you, do not leave us in this plight.'

'But why me?'

'Because you love him!' said Kyrie. 'No-one else loves the Prince as much or as deeply as you. And with love comes respon-sibility. It will be dangerous, but you will have me by your side, and I am a great warrior. If you truly love Boris, you will help us in this. Please, Miss Greta.' Kyrie looked up at her with pleading green eyes, slightly wet with tears of fear for the fate that awaited her and her land without Greta's aid.

There was a long silence before Greta dared to speak. Even as the words fell from her mouth, she didn't really know what she was going to say.

'Ok. I am not brave, and not very capable, but I love Boris, and I have to bring him back. I have to.'

Kyrie smiled. 'Miss Greta, you are both brave and capable, and all the other things you doubt. And your love proves this.

But you will learn. In the meantime, we have to prepare!' She stood up and turned around three times. 'And thank you. You don't know what this means to all of us, to me.' And in a statement of firm friendship and gratitude, Kyrie nuzzled Greta's body with her head.

In which the King makes a speech

Whilst Greta was still asleep and dreaming of where Boris may be hiding, the Kingdom of Cats was in a state of uproar. The Queen had been taken to her chambers, whilst the younger members of the royal family had been sent to their childhood nursery with their tutors and nurses to look after them, keep them safe and occupy their minds. This was really a rather futile task of course, as despite their youth, the two girls and one tom were perfectly aware of the situation. Griselda and Aurora were whimpering quietly, whilst Sweep sat very quietly in the corner of the room, staring blankly at his open book, struggling to hold back his very real and very frightened tears.

The King meanwhile had to consult his advisors. Sitting on his throne in the long grand hallway, so vast that the paintings on the ceiling of great cats through history were barely visible to the naked eye, he began his speech.

'Lords, Ladies and subjects. I am grieved to be forced to make this announcement to you. A great tragedy has occurred in our Kingdom. Together, we must work towards a plan, a solution. I call on you now to help me, your King.'

He paused, letting his courtiers take in his words with muttering and confused looks, and giving himself a few moments to recover himself and appear composed.

'This morning,' he continued, 'my family discovered to our pain and horror that my eldest son, heir to my throne and beloved by all who know him or see him, the Prince Marmaduke Nikolai Boris Blue has been cat-napped by our most deadly and hated foe, the Rat King. I have asked you here today so together we can plan the safe recovery of your Prince, and of my…my son.' With these words the King was forced to stop.

Overcome with emotion, he hid his eyes behind a clenched paw, as the assembled cats in the throne room miaowed their sympathies.

But there wasn't a lot of time to waste in mourning the Prince's kidnap. They had to plan! Ideas were thrown around – perhaps a full scale war against the Rat Kingdom would suffice, a suggestion quickly quashed by the peace-loving royal. Perhaps an arrangement to make a deal with the Rat King would work; an offer of trade or swapping of land. It would be damaging to pride indeed, but surely worth it if it ensured the safety of the Kingdom and of Prince Boris. But nothing could be reasonably decided.

In growing despair, the cats simply could not find a plan that everyone could agree would work. By this point, news of the abduction had spread and the cats who lived far from the palace were travelling to the center of the kingdom to find out exactly what was going on and what was going to happen. The only answer that could reasonably be given was a simple 'I don't know.'

After many hours, the throne room began to fall into an exhausted silence. The Queen Alexandria had joined her husband

and the two sat together on their thrones, paws joined and eyes locked as they awaited a solution. But hope was fading fast.

The King had decided that perhaps now was the time to make a further speech. Yet he had barely risen to his feet when from across the throne room, the door was heard to open.

'I know what must be done,' said a soft, feminine voice, with a barely discernible trace of a foreign accent.

The crowd of cats parted, with great gasps of awe and amazement. For standing in the open doorway was a feline that many of the younger cats had only heard about in legends and at school. She (for indeed it was a she-cat) was white, with upturned green eyes and black and tan patches, beautiful and elegant, yet with a heart as brave as a lion's, and the strength of a leopard.

'Kyrie!' cried the King. 'Kyrie! You have returned!'

Kyrie smiled and bowed her beautiful head. 'Your Highness. A good warrior always knows when to return to her land.'

'Welcome Kyrie,' the Queen said, smiling warmly. 'You do not know how grateful we are to have you here with us, on this most fearful of days.'

It was Kyrie, who you have already met in Greta's kitchen. She was a great and brave warrior, the greatest in the Kingdom of Cats, revered and beloved by all.

'As you know,' she announced to her spellbound audience, 'it has been many years since I have been around the Kingdom of Cats. Yet my love and loyalty to my native land has never left me. Whether protecting my human or those who are in need, I have always been one who wants to help. And it has come to my attention that the ones who need my help now are you, your Royal Highnesses.' With that, she gave a sweeping bow. 'The Prince has been cat-napped. There is only one who can help him, and it is not you, nor I, nor the greatest army. His fate lies in the hands of a young girl, his human. The girl-child Greta is the only one with the strength of heart, courage and love to rescue our future ruler.'

'Of course!' said the King, clutching his wife's paw. 'The human child! How could we have forgotten!'

'The situation is more complex than simply letting her rescue him, Your Highness. The girl is young and nervous, plus unfamiliar with the ways of both our world and that of the Rats, let alone the journey in between. So,' she paused to let her words sink in. 'I propose that I go meet the child and accompany her on the treacherous mission. Without vanity, I am a great warrior and have faced both rats and the perils of the journey to their land on many occasions. I cannot rescue our Prince myself, but I will assist in every way I can, with all my spirit.'

A single tear glistened in the eye of the Queen Alexandria. 'My good Kyrie. You have become a legend in our state for your many acts of bravery and love. And now you offer us this service. You will be much rewarded.'

Kyrie bowed again. 'I do not except reward beyond the pride and honor in knowing I will complete this quest with Greta.'

The King clapped his paws and an atmosphere of muted celebration filled the throne room as a banquet in honor of the returning warrior was prepared and eaten, whilst excited cats young and old clamored around her graceful figure to hear her tales.

To her captive audience, Kyrie told the stories of her travels. From Scotland to America, Africa to Tibet...but it would take a whole other book to fully recount all of Kyrie's marvelous adventures. If you ever go to school in the Kingdom of Cats you will learn about most of them in your history class.

In which Greta faces her first challenge

Greta had no experience of a real-life adventure before. But she had read about them in books and had traveled far and wide in her imagination, so she knew how to prepare. She packed some sandwiches, and bottles of water. She rolled up a spare pair of jeans and a jumper, and a spare t-shirt, and put it all in her rucksack. Finally she added her toothbrush and toothpaste. She was ready to go.

Kyrie nodded approvingly at Greta's preparations. 'We nearly have everything we need,' she said. 'But you have forgotten one important thing. Whenever going on an adventure, especially one that may be dangerous, everyone needs something that will mark them out as a warrior. Something that provides inner strength when it is needed. This must be chosen carefully, for it is the one thing that cannot be advised or chosen by anyone else, and is the most important possession of the warrior. It is from her mascot that her strength is derived, and it is something she can always turn to in times of crisis.'

'Could I ask,' Greta asked, 'what you carry as your mascot?'

'Of course,' said Kyrie. 'I carry an engraving that a cat gave me in Tibet, with the word "peace" written on a tiny piece of wood. The strength of my fight is drawn from a love and desire for peace, not revenge and anger.' Kyrie stretched and revealed the mascot that she wore on a collar around her neck. 'So choose wisely Greta. It determines a lot about your adventure.'

Greta nodded and returned upstairs to find her mascot. She felt, after the gravity and beauty of Kyrie's choice, that she could not afford to let her guide down. But it was hard! Hard to know what was most precious to her, what would help her in her fight. This kind of thing had never happened to her before.

And then, passing by the corner of her dressing table, she realized what it was that she should take. She picked up a locket belonging to her great-grandmother that had been passed down a few generations until it had reached her. Inside was a photo of Boris as a kitten, and a photo of her. From her family's past, her own life and the purpose of her mission she could gain her strength. She hurried downstairs, told Kyrie her choice and the two smiled warmly at each other. They were ready to go.

'Is it a long way?' asked Greta, after the two of them had been walking through the forests behind her house for a good many hours.

Greta had never before realized how vast the woods were, which she suspected had something to do with the fact that she had never walked through them with a member of the animal world before. The ways of the forest were far greater and more significant than human built paths would have you believe. She had become aware of so many things in the last few hours that she would never have seen without Kyrie. They had passed towns and villages of mice and voles, the boating communities in the brooks and streams, the bats and birds working the telegraph service, the tunnels that led to the underground cities of what Kyrie referred to darkly as 'the dogs' but which Greta understood to mean foxes and badgers. When asked this, Kyrie had just spat and said how all dogs were just one big pain to her. So Greta decided not to pursue the subject and inform her that badgers weren't, in actual fact, dogs at all. She felt that Kyrie was someone you just didn't enter into arguments with.

Greta was amazed by the beauty of the forest that she had lived so close to for so many years. It felt like she was seeing it for the first time. They had walked through shrubs and under oaks and chestnuts, sycamores and ash, every tree she could think of. The ground under them was moving with friendly bugs and the air was buzzing with the sounds of bees and birdsong. The moss under her feet cushioned her every step, as ferns and overhanging branches brushed against her bare arms in a pleasantly tickling and scratchy manner. After the first green stage of the forest they had passed a meadow filled with wild flowers and long sweeping grasses, where small mice scurried about their feet (Kyrie was very good and claimed she wasn't hungry), and rabbits and hares bounded across their path.

Along from the meadow stood the evergreens, tall and haunting, where soft brown earth and leaves lay underfoot. They stretched so tall that the tops were invisible, providing a sheltering canopy overhead. Unlike the busy nature of the wood and the meadow, here it was still and quiet. The only sound came from their footsteps and occasional conversation. Then the leafy green trees returned, and once more they were back amidst the wild buzz of forest life. Greta felt that they must have been walking for miles, and she had to admit that she was getting tired and rather hungry. Suddenly, Kyrie stopped in her tracks, circled herself three times and sat down.

'Here we are then,' she said, enjoying the feeling of not being on her feet.

Greta sat down beside her. They were underneath a huge oak with a massive canopy of bright green leaves. Acorns were budding on every branch. Scattered on the ground around them, nestling in the roots, were great piles of golden and red and orange autumn leaves. The ground glowed with the warm colors, just as the sky dazzled in green.

'Here we are where?' Greta asked, making herself comfortable between two vastly wide roots.

'At the staircase. We're early, but that's ok, as I'm hungry! I really think it's time to crack open some food.'

Greta nodded, and decided to keep her confusion quiet. As far as she could see there was no staircase, nor had she ever known any reason why you'd be "early" to reach a staircase. She reasoned to herself that all would be explained to her eventually, that Kyrie was wise and disliked to be pestered, and right now food was their priority. She opened the knapsack and gave Kyrie her chicken and some milk which she lapped up, whilst Greta

27

had some juice and rice salad. Chewing over her food, she started thinking about where she was and what would happen to her. For the first time in the day, she felt frightened. It was strange. She had been swept away in the excitement of meeting Kyrie, so that the actual realization of what she was doing had failed to dawn on her. But now her head became rather too full of the fact that Boris was missing, she had to rescue him from a Rat King, and she was under the protection of a warrior cat who she didn't know, travelling to she didn't know where. Her parents were in Botswana, no-one knew where she was and it all seemed very dangerous and frightening. She couldn't stop now. But she wished she felt less scared.

Kyrie watched her, seeing the path of expressions travel across her face.

'You're getting frightened, aren't you?' she asked, her voice full of kindness.

'Oh, n...no, it's, it's fine.'

Kyrie laughed. 'Silly you! It's okay to be scared. We are all scared sometimes. And what we have asked of you is frightening. Not just that, but it is daunting and hard to understand. Yet, what you must keep remembering is that you were chosen for a reason, Greta. And that reason is simple. You can do this. You are the only one who is truly able to. The Kingdom of Cats has many warriors, yet we knew that you would be the only one who could succeed. And we wouldn't have asked it of you if we didn't believe that. But what matters is that you believe it too. You have to believe in yourself, Greta. In you, and in your strength and your bravery, and in your love for Boris. Only then can you overcome fear. Being scared is natural. And so is freedom from it.'

Greta had a few tears in her eyes, but managed a smile. 'You're right Kyrie. But it's hard. It is hard to think of myself as brave.'

'I know. But you are courageous. Every day in your life you show bravery in daring to be yourself. You are strong in your character and in staying true to yourself. And that is braver than fighting ten thousand rats single-handedly. Hold on to that, for it is what makes you wise and magical.

'Now I am going to explain to you what happens next. To reach the next stage of our journey, we have to climb the staircase of autumn leaves, which builds here in around five minutes. At that time, the wind blows at the tree from the east, pulling up the leaves that we're sitting on and forming a spiral that leads to Cloud-Top Land. We have to climb up it so that we can continue our travels.'

'But how do we climb leaves?' asked Greta, feeling nervous once more.

Kyrie smiled slowly. 'Through trust. To travel up the leaves, you have to trust that you won't fall. You have to believe in yourself. You have to have faith in your courage and ability. Trust the leaves beneath your feet. If you believe that you can walk the staircase, then you will stay up and climb it successfully.'

'And if not?'

Kyrie shrugged. 'I think you know the answer to that. But hurry, there's no time for pondering. Here she comes!'

As she spoke, a mammoth gust of wind pulled at Greta's hair and made her jump back. She quickly began to stuff their belongings back into the bag, whilst she watched the magnificent sight unfold in front of her eyes.

As the wind blew, the carpet of gold and red and orange leaves that had lain so peacefully under their feet was whipped into a fury. It flew up into the air around them as the wind blew the leaves round and round, higher and higher, spiraling into the sky to create a golden-red staircase of autumn leaves.

'It's so beautiful!' Greta cried out in amazement. She felt that never in her life had she seen anything so wonderful.

'Come on then!' Kyrie said, and with a graceful bound she landed on the first step of leaves. They supported her weight perfectly and she began to climb.

'Ok,' Greta murmured. 'I can do this. I believe in myself. I really do believe I can do this.' She hesitated for a moment longer. 'Well. Here goes!'

With a slightly clumsy leap, she found herself in the air walking over the spiraling leaves. 'I'm doing it!' she squealed. 'Look Kyrie! I'm really doing it!'

'Of course you are,' Kyrie said. 'I never doubted you would!'

Overwhelmed with happiness at her ability to walk on the floating leaves, Greta ran quickly up the stairs; trusting that for each step the leaves, wind and her own self-belief would stop her from falling. But as she got ever higher, nerves started to creep into the back of her mind. What if she stopped believing, she thought. What then? Would she fall? Could she fall? She was so high up and she had no idea what lay beneath her. Or above her for that matter. Self-belief was so shifting. What if she took one step without...

'AHHHHH!' she screamed, as she stepped forward to find nothing but air beneath her. 'Kyrie!' she shouted, 'help me!'

But Kyrie was too far away to really hear her over the rush of the wind and the rustling of the leaves that drowned out her cries.

Greta found herself clutching onto the leaves with her legs dangling into the nothing beneath her. She knew she had to trust herself and believe in her ability to get back on the staircase. But having fallen, she had lost so much of what little self-belief she had anyway. Hanging there, she wrestled with the voices that told her she was in danger, as she struggled to recover the pride and bravery that had been with her minutes before, skipping up the leaves.

She could feel her grasp on the leaves, the only thing holding her up, getting weaker and weaker. Slowly, her mind began to give up. She had been wrong, Kyrie had been wrong. She wasn't able to do this. They had made a mistake. Tiredness swept over her as she felt the leaves begin, slowly, slowly, to slip from beneath her hands.

Just then, she felt a burning sensation right against her chest. She looked down to see her mascot, her locket, glowing red against her skin, as the ache in her chest got worse. With a flash of clarity, she realized what was happening. She had forgotten where she was, what she was doing. She had to rescue Boris. She had to! She loved Boris, and he had always been there for her. And a bunch of leaves and some silly hesitating doubts weren't going to get between her and those that she loved!

With a massive push of will, she grabbed hold of the leaves that began to feel steadier under her now unflinching hands. She pulled herself up, and the leaves bore her weight. Clutching hold of her locket, she got onto her feet and stood firm on the path of leaves below her. Then, with a look of sheer strength and determination on her face, she began to run, faster and faster, quicker than she had ran the 100m race at school. Her feet became fairy light, skipping and jumping over the path that pushed her higher and higher on the wind, whilst the rustle of the leaves wished her good luck and love.

The ground shrank below her but she refused to look down, holding her locket and thinking of Boris. She thought of the strength that Kyrie had told her she possessed, and laughed at the stupidity of her doubts. All that mattered now was the overwhelming importance of her mission. And soon enough she could see Kyrie waiting at the top, as with a final push she landed beside her on what appeared to be a soft and sandy beach. The leaves fell beneath her as the wind died down, collecting themselves back below the great oak. And there they lay still, waiting for the next gust of wind that would build the staircase.

Greta smiled.

In which Greta travels through Cloud-Top Land

'Thew!' cried Kyrie. 'Well done Greta! What did I tell you?'

Greta nodded, smiling. 'I know. I thought I'd lost it, but then...'

'I had every faith. And that is the first step. Once one more person has faith in you, the easier it becomes to discover faith in yourself.' She paused to nuzzle Greta's face. 'But really, there is no time to lose. We have a long way to go and not enough moments in the day. So, come on, shake yourself down and let's keep moving!'

Although she felt tired and really wanted to rest for as long as she could, Greta obediently followed Kyrie's instructions. She shook the leaves from her hair and clothes and stood up. As she did so, she began to fully appreciate the splendor that surrounded her. In her fear and excitement in climbing the staircase, she hadn't paid much attention to where exactly it was that they were going.

They had reached the land above the treetops. Here, the clouds settle at the uppermost tips of the tallest trees, which is why you often can't see the tops of the trees when you're walking in the forest. The land wasn't land as we understand it here in the human world, rather it was a swirling, sweet mist. It seemed so light and moist under her feet, yet it held her aloft so that she didn't sink into it. In this white maze you could see the heads of the trees poking their way through the clouds. From below they were so high and imposing, yet here they were only about the same height as she was. Everything was silver and green and it was the most beautiful landscape she had ever seen.

'Kyrie!' she said. 'It's incredible.'

Kyrie shrugged. 'It does have a certain charm to it, I admit. But I must say it isn't the greatest place I have seen. Still, it is rather lovely.'

Greta didn't argue. After all, Kyrie must have seen many marvelous sights whereas her own experience was rather more limited.

They walked a long time in the cloudy land, feet and ankles slightly damp from the mist. Greta was in awe of the landscape but Kyrie strode on with firm concentration. As they went past the village of swallows and swifts, Greta remembered that she had been taught at school that these birds rarely touch the ground. But now she learnt that the reason we never see them walking around in our world is because they did all their resting here, in Cloud-Top Land.

Further along the route they came to the villages of seabirds, who retired here when the days and weeks and months of skimming over the sea forced them to seek a few days of rest in the Cloud-Top towns. Everyone greeted Kyrie and Greta with welcoming respect, something that surprised Greta a little. Not because she was shocked that fellow creatures would respect Kyrie, just that she had never imagined that cats would receive a warm reception from birds. Yet, everywhere they went, whoever they met, they would rush down to greet Kyrie, offer the travelers a drink or something to eat – offers which they always accepted. In this way, Greta met the gannets and albatrosses, shared dinner with a family of swallows and a commune of swifts, discussed geo-politics with a debating team of razorbills and terns, and had conversations about the problem of melting icecaps with almost every type of migrating bird she had heard of (and a few she hadn't).

As the two traveled across Cloud-Top Land, they were well-received by all and depended on the kindness of strangers to help them on their way. Despite the long walk, the whole journey had such a friendly and carnival atmosphere to it that Greta forgot to feel tired or afraid. She was just happy to listen to the talk of the birds, soak in the gorgeous scenery around her and enjoy the tasty food and drink on offer. Although she had felt it necessary to turn down the grub and worm stew cooked by the swallows (opting instead for some of her own emergency supplies) she ate well on fish caught fresh from the oceans and rivers – sardines, salmon, trout and cod; as well as the weird drink concoctions invented by the birds: dandelion and daisy juice, berry cordials and distilled sea water.

Everywhere she went, Greta felt that as opposed to being on a dangerous rescue mission, she was on a happy and friendly holiday, exploring new landscapes and enjoying good food, drink and company.

But where was it they were heading? Greta asked this same question to Kyrie a few days into their trip.

'To the port,' Kyrie replied.

'Oh,' Greta said. She paused. She was fairly used by now to Kyrie's sometimes frustratingly short answers. 'What port would that be?' She fancied the reply was not going to be Liverpool, or Bristol.

'The Port of the Milky Sea,' was the next answer. 'The Milky Sea is, unsurprisingly, the waters owned by the cats. Although, it isn't water; the sea is made of milk. It links the Cloud-Top Land, where the birds live, to the Land of Mice. Beyond the Land of Mice we will find the Rat Kingdom. The Milky Sea is owned by cats, and shows the populations that surround it how we are in fact a peace-loving kingdom. Although the necessity of nature forces us to sometimes eat mice and birds, we would never dream of falling into conflict with their lands. The whole idea of nature is harmony.'

Greta could see this being one of the times when Kyrie would share some of her famed knowledge and wisdom, and listened carefully.

'Many humans have trouble,' she said, 'understanding the working of nature. It is for this reason that the human world, as they see it, is in trouble. That is what the birds meant when they talked about the polar ice caps. But we animals, we have a very different relationship with each other and with nature. We understand the necessity of harmony in living close to each other. For example, each animal in the non-human world appreciates the value of the food chain. This means that, although no bird would willingly give its life to be cat food, if it loses the chase, then it is understood that it dies without being waste. Similarly a plant understands that it is food for a rabbit, a grub understands that it is food for a bird. We do not invade the lands of our neighboring animals to feed. But on fair and neutral ground, hunting to eat is permitted. When I walk through the Cloud-Top Land, the birds are not afraid because we know that neither of us can attack the other on their own territory.'

'But what about the rats taking Boris?'

Kyrie sighed. 'Not all animals obey the rules' she said. 'Just as in the human world many are good whilst some are cruel, so it is in the animal world. The rats are a greedy and wicked race that breaks the rules. But most animals are good and respect the balance of this natural harmony. If they didn't,' Kyrie here paused and shrugged. 'If they didn't, then the world would fall apart.'

'So, what have the humans done wrong?' Greta asked. She dreaded the answer, but was curious to know the animal world's perspective. The more she knew, she decided, the more equipped she was to complete her rescue mission.

'Greta, you are a human child, and you are brave and beautiful in spirit. Many men and women are like you. That is something you must bear in mind, as what I am going to say may otherwise seem cruel. But you must be able to appreciate that many humans are wicked. They do not understand nature's harmony.

'Here in our animal world, we see how food and energy must be shared between all of us, so that each breed and species can survive side by side. It is for this reason that we live happily together. But this is not the case with humans, all the time. So some humans go hungry, whilst others eat. And there is fighting and people feeling sad. In the animal world, this doesn't happen.'

Greta did not reply. She knew that what Kyrie said was true. Humans, despite thinking that they were better than the animals around them, had not found the harmony and balance that she had seen governing the lives of the creatures she had met. Humans all too often were not afraid to hurt and steal for no good reason.

Kyrie smiled. 'Greta, I don't need to tell you that this is not all humans. Just as not all animals live according to nature's balance. The mice are at war with each other as we speak. But we can learn from the different manners and behaviors of each other. That is how we grow and learn.' She nuzzled Greta affectionately. 'And here we are. The Port of the Milky Sea.'

In which Greta visits the Port of the Milky Sea

Greta looked up and caught her breath. The view was incredible. Lapping at the cloudy shores was a deep milky and silver ocean that stretched for miles around. As the sun shone up through the clouds beneath them, it illuminated the sea bright white, bathing everything around it in a deep, rich light. It tinted Greta, Kyrie and everyone at the port with a yellow glow. Everyone and everything was shining and beautiful.

'It's unbelievable,' said Greta. Kyrie nodded in agreement, although her enthusiasm for her surroundings wasn't as intense as Greta's. Kyrie had seen most of these sights before, and many more wonders besides during her travels and adventures. She claimed that no landscape was as intense and amazing as the Russian mountains and the steppes and deserts of Siberia.

But she understood how when seeing it for the first time, the sight of the Milky Sea was something special.

It wasn't just the sight of the ocean that was brilliant to Greta. She was standing in the center of one of the busiest ports in the world. Liverpool and Bristol – they had nothing on this. Scurrying past her came mice in uniforms boarding army and naval ships ('the mice are at war,' murmured Kyrie); albatrosses with their passengers of voles and shrews and other small rodents cruising into land; rabbits organizing boat tours to the Curdled Islands for holidaying hares; stores selling buttermilk and cream and yoghurt and cheese, as well as cafés selling milky drinks of every kind.

'Some sustenance, I think,' announced Kyrie, licking her lips delicately. 'Then we had better find a boat.'

The pair wandered through the hustle and bustle to an ice-cream parlor, ran by a very round and furry cat who hailed originally from Italy, and who was now known to be the proprietor of the most famous and delicious ice-cream parlor in the animal world.

'Mamma mia! It is the warrior Kyrie! And you mia bella, must be the girl-child Greta! I welcome you three times over to my humble and unworthy shop! Whatever you order will be on the house. Now, I need to know! What is your pleasure?'

'Giorgio, it has been too long!' Kyrie said. 'I've missed you. Greta, please let me introduce Primo Lorenzo Giorgio White, or Giorgio. He makes the best ice cream in the Kingdom of Cats. His ice cream is loved by the King and Prince, and today you will try it. What do you fancy?'

Greta chose clotted cream in a cone, whilst Kyrie had Neapolitan. The two were treated as guests of honor in the parlor. Giorgio fussed over them and made it known to all the other customers eating there who his VIP guests were, much to Greta's embarrassment.

The delicious ice-cream never seemed to dribble and melt down its cone, and the last mouthful tasted as crisp and cold as the first. But there was no time to rest. As soon as they had finished eating, Kyrie leapt up and led Greta back out to the busy port, in search of a boat.

Everywhere they went in the Port of the Milky Sea they were greeted with love and joy. The news of Boris' cat-nap had spread, as had the news of the proposed rescue, and there was no shortage of offers of suitable transport. Eagles offered lifts high in the air, turtles offered their backs as floats whilst the rabbits suggested the use of one of their chartered tour boats to make the journey. The warring factions of mice showed one thing they agreed on at least; they both wanted Greta and Kyrie to use one of their ships. But Kyrie politely refused all their kindnesses. She had, she told Greta, already someone in mind who would help them.

At the end of the road that ran along the stretch of the port, there stood a small and slightly run down shack. It was made of wood. Each plank was at odds with the other; the windows were uneven and dusty and the roof looked like it had seen better days. But at the sight of it, Kyrie's normally impassive face broke open into a huge beaming smile and tears lit up her clear and pretty eyes. She ran over to the door and knocked on it three times.

After a wait, the latch clicked and the door opened, revealing a very old and yet still handsome mi-ke cat – the same breed as Kyrie herself.

Kyrie flung herself at his ancient frame. 'Grandpa!' she shouted, as she started to cry. 'I knew I'd find you here!'

'Kyrie,' he said, patting her gently as he held her close to him. 'My little Kyrie!'

'Greta,' she said, pulling back. 'Let me introduce to you my grandfather, Uchida Haruki Samurai Mi-ke, or Sam, as he is more commonly known. Grandpa, this is Greta.'

'I know who you are my dear,' he said, laughing merrily. 'Why, all of us cats know your name!'

'I'm pleased to meet you,' Greta replied, shaking him by the paw. 'It is always an honor to meet someone who is a friend of Kyrie's.' (Greta was beginning to pick up the way cats spoke to one another).

'Come in, come in,' he said, smiling all the while. 'I'll warm some milk.'

The three made their way into the tiny little house. As they entered, Greta saw it was decorated with all kinds of fishing objects, from rods and ropes to models of boats; interspersed with Japanese artefacts that she recognized from her father's museum.

'We cannot stop long, Grandpa,' Kyrie said, sipping her warm milk. 'We have to press on with our journey to rescue the Prince Marmaduke Nikolai Boris Blue.' (Greta was also getting more used to hearing Boris referred to in this way.) 'We came to ask if we could borrow your boat.'

At her words, the old cat started to rock with laughter. He giggled and chortled, until Kyrie began to look rather cross. 'Grandpa-san! Please appreciate the seriousness of this matter! The Crown Prince is in danger, we need to cross the Milky Sea, and we hoped to borrow your boat! Why are you laughing?'

'Oh my sweet child, Kyrie! Borrow my boat indeed! Have you forgotten our family honor and laws? No-one borrows the boat of Uchida Haruki Samurai Mi-ke – san. I will captain you myself. Let not my frame or age deceive you, young agile one. I will captain my boat and take you safely across the sea. I will catch you fish and bring your milk, and together we will travel to the warring Land of Mice. With me as your captain, you will have no fear of threat or injury, however old or frail I may appear.'

Sam seemed to grow in strength and grandeur as he spoke, his pride for his boat and his sailing ability shining in his face.

'Very well,' Kyrie replied. 'Forgive me for any doubt I may have had. But let us go now, we have delayed long enough.'

If Sam's house had seemed rather rickety and rackety, then his boat was its complete opposite. The wood shone like burnished

gold and the sail fluttered in the wind, bright and clean. It was spick and span and built with such obvious love and attention that Greta felt compelled to stroke its shining and glowing sides.

'She's beautiful,' she said.

Sam nodded proudly. 'Sayuri was built by me many, many years ago, as soon as I came of age. She has served me well ever since, as she will today.'

'My grandfather is one of the world's greatest fisherman,' Kyrie added, the pride in her voice evident.

Greta smiled warmly in response, and with his help, boarded the boat. They were off!

'It is a long way across the sea,' said Sam, as he pulled the boat out of the harbor and into the open water/milk. 'But I will guide you across it safely. First, however, I must ask my beautiful granddaughter to tell me where she has been all these years. Come, sweet child, I want to hear it all. You have kept an old tom waiting too long. Where have you been? What have you seen?'

'Yes, do tell us, Kyrie,' Greta said. 'I would love to hear of your adventures!'

Kyrie smiled. 'Okay. I will begin.'

In which Kyrie tells many stories

'I left the Kingdom of Cats when I was barely grown up, the cat age of eighteen. Which in your human years, Greta, would have made me around three years old. In my youth I had proven my bravery many times over. I was a champion, winning prizes and respect in tournaments. With my strength and intelligence it was only natural that I went into the Battle Cats division of the Protective Actions Warriors' Society (also known as "PAWS", for short).

'Yet, once there, I was unhappy. I was a strong fighter and a good sports player. I was smart and bright and I was a highly skilled warrior. But the life didn't suit me. I found it too regimented. The generals were in constant fear of attack from human or rat, yet they were unwilling to look closely at how to create peace. After winning the respect of the royal family and other leading cats, I left PAWS and began to travel. I wanted to take the skills I had learnt in fighting and tournaments to pursue an understanding of peace.

'This began with my travels to the northern points of Scotland, where I was aware that there was a conflict between hawk and falcon.' Here she paused. 'Greta, I told you earlier that we animals all try and live together in a natural harmony. Most animals succeed, but sometimes things go wrong, as we are now seeing in the battle between Brown and White mice, or even with the cat-napping of our Prince. So it was with the hawk and falcon.

'The hawks and the falcons were fighting because the hawks felt that the falcons were trying to invade the neutral feeding ground, depriving the hawks of their food. It was nonsense of course, as most arguments are. So I decided to try and offer my own opinion with the hope that I could end the battle. And after much talking and no more killing, it was decided that each day they would take it in turns to hunt and then share their bounty, so that neither side would lose food.

'This was my first experience of using peace and conversation to solve a problem and end a battle, and I was successful. This spurred me on to travel further abroad.

'I continued going north until I reached a harbor and jumped on a ship to America. It took me to New York where I went sight-seeing, before I hitched lifts on a variety of cars and trains across the country. Eventually I had gone right from the east coast of NYC to the west coast in California. I headed to Hollywood to see what all the fuss was about, and lived the wild life for a few months. I worked as an extra in the movies, and got to see the glitz and the glamor of the town. But it meant nothing to me. It was fun, no-one could deny that. But I felt there something missing. So I decided it was time to move on.

'After Hollywood I decided to try and discover something about my cat roots, so I took up with a troupe of desert cougars. They lived in Arizona, and I learnt about the delicate balance that exists between humans and animals. With the cougars I saw how people and cats should live side by side and that danger only occurred when one species invaded another's space. When humans tried to destroy the cougars' home and fighting broke out, I decided it was once more time to move further on. I still had much to see and learn.

'And so it was that from America I ended up on another ship, heading to South Africa. It's a country that is considered a great place of learning for cats. I was excited. And the continent of Africa! The homeland of our Queen's family, and the home of lions and leopards and cheetahs – these animals would surely teach me so much. And I was not disappointed.

'On the vast plains in that beautiful country, I met all the creatures I had heard so much about. The lions taught me the wisdom of hunting, the balance between predator and prey. I learnt from them about the respect between all animals that forms the natural harmony of the food chain. I traveled north, until I reached Kenya. Here I met the cheetahs who taught me how to use my body for strength and speed. I learnt how to control my muscles and heart to increase my ability to chase and hunt. I found a speed and strength I never realized I had. From the leopards I learnt stealth – how to stay hidden and how to observe the rest of the world from the treetops. These days were some of the greatest I have ever spent.

'When I felt that I had learnt all I could from this vast continent, it was once more time to continue my travels. I continued heading east, until I arrived in India. What a place! Here I met the tigers and lived with them for a while, and discovered the lore of the jungle. I learned about the history of the tigers, and in the forests I discovered more about nature's harmony.

'But once more I was learning, as I had in Africa and America, about the differences between humans, between rich and poor, between fighting and peace. In search of more information about peace, I traveled north to the stillness of the mountains where the Buddhist cats lived, and I stayed with them for a year or so. They taught me about the harmony that must exist between all living things. They showed me how peace is achieved by us all working as one and not against each other. They live in quietness surrounded by beauty, they hurt nothing and quarrel with no-one. I learnt from them that whilst it is okay to be angry at injustice; that anger can quickly lead to hate, a hatred that is destructive. I discovered instead how to be calm and how to listen.

'I felt that in the mountains I had nearly completed my education. Yet I was aware that learning was a lifelong process, which each future experience would enrich.

'I had come so far east that the next logical step was to travel to the land of my ancestors.' Here she paused to smile lovingly at her grandfather. 'Japan! I was so happy to be there. I went straight to Tokyo where I was amazed and awed by my surroundings. After the beautiful silence of the monasteries, the hustle and bustle and excitement of the city was overwhelming. I moved in with a student called Sumire who wrote stories and played lots of music on a record player. She would tell me about the books she was reading and the thoughts she had. It gave me a good insight into the human mind and to this day she is the human I look after. We have an arrangement that we both have our freedom, so that we'll see each other when we see each other. Together we took many walks, and I enjoyed being in Japan.

'But even though the call of my homeland was strong, I felt I still had more to see. So Sumire and I discussed the problem and she let me go, so long as I promised to come and visit from time to time. I traveled back west and arrived in Russia. Never have I seen a place like that! The beauty of the endless mountains, the emptiness, the trees, the feeling that you are alone in the world – nowhere was like Russia. It was a place I will always treasure in my heart.

'After Russia, after all my travels and educations, I felt that I had come close to what I had hoped to achieve, to see the world and learn from what I saw. So I returned to Tokyo and to Sumire. We were overjoyed to be together again. She had started to write a new story, and we would sit on her balcony, eating rice and reading it together. Then the news of the cat-napping of Prince Boris arrived, and it was time to nuzzle her goodbye again. And here I am, with you.'

'My goodness!' said Greta. 'You have been everywhere! And you've learnt so much.'

'That is what makes the great warrior,' Sam said, nodding solemnly. 'It is not skill with the sword or pistol. It is the knowledge to avoid the fight. But dear granddaughter, your stories have lasted long enough. We have reached your destination. You are at the warring Land of Mice.'

In which a war is fought and ended

After the beauty of the lands and seas that Greta and Kyrie had traveled through, the Land of Mice was a terrible sight. Compared to the lushness of the busy port and the mysterious sights of Cloud-Top Land, the mice's home was plain, dusty and bare of trees. It was a war zone, with barbed wire criss-crossing the empty landscape. Greta winced at the sight. She associated mice with the cute little animals that sometimes Boris brought in, or the pets some of her friends had kept. Not with this war-torn, destroyed land.

'It's awful' she said.

Sam and Kyrie nodded in sad sympathy. 'Greta,' Kyrie said. 'There are some things you need to know before we set off across this land. As you can see, the war has destroyed the landscape and harmed many of the inhabitants. It is a dangerous place but with me you will be safe, I promise that.'

'But what is this war? How did it start?'

Sam rolled his eyes. 'The same reason all wars start. Stupid debates. Petty disagreements turning to hate.'

'Grandfather is right,' said Kyrie. 'This disastrous war started for the falsest and most dangerous of reasons. You remember how I told you that most of us here in the animal kingdom live side by side? Well, sometimes this goes wrong, sometimes animals break the trust and stop caring about living in harmony. Humans were the first, then the rats, and now the mice. It happened one day that the White mice came to the decision that they no longer liked the Brown mice. For the silliest of reasons! They decided that because they slept in beds of sawdust they were better than the Brown mice, who sleep in beds of leaves. The White mice said that sawdust was cleaner, and therefore they were the better mouse. Of course, the Brown mice got very cross about this, and a huge row between the community leaders erupted. Both sides started to tease each other, and it all started to get out of control. And then, the fighting began. The war has raged on ever since. And all because of a petty argument over who slept on the better bed.'

Greta sat still and listened. The situation was horrible. Why did the mice hate each other for such silly reasons? And why did it have to cause such destruction?

'It's so stupid,' she said. 'So, the White mice decided that they were better than the Brown mice because of the beds they sleep in? And this ridiculous belief has caused all of this suffering?'

Kyrie and Sam nodded.

'Kyrie, you are a warrior! You can't let this happen! How come no-one has done anything to try and help?'

'What can you do, Greta?' Kyrie said. 'They won't stop fighting, and we cannot fight mice, it's too unfair, too uneven. They wouldn't listen to us.'

Greta set her face firmly. 'We have to do something. We are going to see the army leaders. We are going to stop this.'

Sam smiled admiringly at the young girl. 'She has your spirit, Granddaughter,' he said, pride in his voice. 'You must do as she says. She has come this far, she is the one to rescue the Prince. We must support her in this fight.'

'I can do it, of course I can.' Greta breathed deeply, surprised at the force in her voice. She had no idea she had such determination, or strength. But she felt such an overwhelming certainty that this was something she could do, something she could achieve. Just as every passing minute she felt more confident that she would be able to save Boris.

Kyrie shrugged. 'If that is what you want, then of course we will. But for now, we must say goodbye to my grandfather.' She turned to him, her eyes full of love and tears. 'We'll see you soon, won't we?'

'Pah!' he said, laughing. 'Soon? I will be waiting here for you and Greta when she brings our beloved and esteemed Prince

Boris back home to us. Together we will sail across the sea and go on to the Kingdom of Cats. Now, you go and tell those mice to stop this war, fight those rats and save our future King!'

Greta laughed. 'Sam, thank you so much! We'll see you soon.'

Kyrie hugged her grandfather tight. 'We will see you soon, Grandpa.' And with that they parted, to start the journey across the Land of Mice.

As they left Sam bobbing in his boat on the Milky Sea, Greta and Kyrie started to make their way across the war torn Land of Mice. They stumbled and tripped over the uneven, bomb-cratered land, whilst ahead of them they could hear the booming of guns and cannons, the shouts of commands and the cries of the injured.

Greta could see that the land had once been green and lush. But now, instead of towering trees there were just stumps. Where there had been thriving and vibrant towns and communities, there were just ruins. Brown and White mice lived separately in tumble-down shelters and camps, wary and angry with one another. As they pressed on, Greta saw White mice cross the ruined streets to avoid walking near the Brown mice. She overheard a Brown mother mouse scolding her child for waving at a White mouse former friend. A lump formed in her throat as she saw firsthand what petty prejudices can do. As she took in the devastation around her, she became more and more uneasy about the task she had decided to take on. This war was dangerous and vicious. What if Kyrie was right and she could do nothing?

'No,' she muttered to herself. 'Look what that kind of thinking did last time. Why, I nearly fell down the staircase of autumn leaves! I can do this. I just have to put my mind to it. I just have to focus on what I need to do.'

'Here we are,' Kyrie interrupted her thoughts. 'This is the major battle field.'

Greta looked around her. Two huge armies of White and

Brown mice were facing each other. They held their guns and spears aloft; ready for the pounce. The ground they stood upon shuddered under the marching of paws, and the air rang with the squeaks and shrieks of their battle cries.

'Are you sure you want to do this?' Kyrie asked in a low voice.

Greta took a deep breath, braced herself, and nodded slowly. 'Yes. This is something I really believe in.'

'Okay. Well, I'm going to get their attention. It's going to be loud, so get ready!'

'MMMIIIIIIIIIIIIIIIIIIIIIIIIIIIIIIIIIIIIIIIIIIIIIAAA AAAAAAAAAAAAAOOOOOOOOOOOOOOOWWWWWWWW' Kyrie screeched, her voice breaking over the sounds of war and weapons. At the sound, a silence fell over the field as every beady pair of mouse eyes turned in their direction. Greta's heart was in her mouth. She realized she had never been so afraid in her life.

Kyrie spoke first. 'I am Miu Sumire Kyrie Mi-ke, a warrior of the Kingdom of Cats and ambassador of the King Marmaduke Nikolai Whiskers Blue, he who is ruler of the Kingdom of Cats, Terror of Mice, Menace of Birds and Nemesis of Hounds, Surveyor of the Peace, Emperor of the Feline Race and Lord of

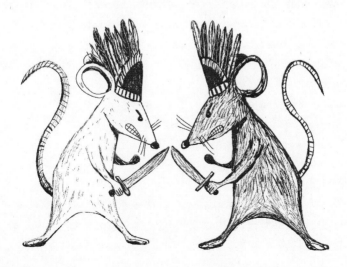

the surrounding lands. This is the girl-child Greta, protector of the Prince Marmaduke Nikolai Boris Blue. We would like to speak with the leaders of the White and Brown mice.'

The leader of the White Mice and the leader of the Brown Mice both stepped forward.

'I am Snowy, Ruler of the White Mice of the sawdust beds. I accept the request for audience, however I will not speak to my foe, that leader of my enemy army.'

When he had finished, the leader of the Brown Mice stepped forward.

'And I am Riverbank, commander of the Brown Mice of the leafy beds. I too accept the request for audience however I will not speak to my foe, that commander of my enemy army.'

'We thank you,' Kyrie nodded gratefully with grace. She looked to Greta, who realized this was her cue to start.

'I,' she began. Her voice sounded small and young next to the powerful cry of Kyrie. 'I wanted to speak to you. I wanted to ask you why you are fighting.'

'Because we are the superior mice!' replied Snowy, his voice rising in anger. 'We sleep on clean beds of sawdust, not on muddy leaves. We are the better mice!'

'Rubbish!' shouted back Riverbank. 'Leafy beds are clean and soft, and far nicer and cozier than your scratchy sawdust! You just think you are better than us!'

'Is this true?' Greta asked Snowy. 'Did you attack the Brown mice because you think you are better than they are? Simply because of how they build their beds?'

'Indeed,' said Snowy. 'And right we are.'

'That's very interesting,' said Greta.

'It is not interesting!' said Riverbank. 'It is a war! It is a disgrace!'

'Oh no, I agree, I really do,' said Greta. 'It is just interesting that Snowy believes that White mice are better due to the materials they use to build their beds, and chose to tease you about it. And it's interesting that you have used fighting and violence to try and disprove his claim.'

The mice looked at each other, confused. Greta knew then that she had them.

'You see, a lot of people tease me because they think I'm different to them,' she continued.

'But you seem so nice!' Snowy and Riverbank interrupted her. It was the first time they had both spoken together and agreed with one another for five long years. They gave each other a scowl. But, Kyrie thought, that was the first step...

'Well, it is kind of you to say so,' said Greta, pleased to see her plan was working. 'However, there are some people who disagree. Now, the girls in my school, they laughed at my hair and teased me. They refused to be my friend. They told me my clothes were strange, and that I had weird parents. They wouldn't speak to me.'

'Because they didn't like your hair?' they asked. Again, they glared at each other as they heard their voices speak in unison.

'That's right. They looked at me, and decided that they didn't like what they saw.'

'Before they even spoke to you?' they both asked.

'Before they even spoke to me. They decided that because of the way I looked, they didn't want to be my friends, and chose instead to be nasty.' She paused. 'It's called bullying.'

'Ridiculous,' they said, both shaking their heads.

'Oh it is, it is. And it's horrible. I walk through the halls at my school and they throw things at me. They call me names and laugh at me. But they have never spoken to me, they've never tried to get to know me. They just decided they didn't like me because they didn't like my hair.'

As Greta spoke, feelings of guilt and remorse started to spread across the armies of White and Brown mice. They began to think that maybe, just maybe, they were doing to each other what the bullies had been doing to Greta.

'And it isn't just bullies being mean to me at school.' She searched her memory for what she'd been taught in history lessons. 'In the human world, men and women were put in prison and badly hurt, because one group of people didn't like their skin color, or the country they came from, or their religion. Without even trying to talk to them first.'

She stopped here, and let her words sink in. The mice were listening and thinking in silence, as they stood on the dusty battlefield.

'Why are you telling us this?' Snowy asked, in a very, very small voice.

'I just thought you might be interested,' she replied.

The silence continued.

'White Mouse Snowy,' Riverbank said, his voice surprisingly strong and steady considering it was the first time he had spoken to a White mouse in five years. 'I believe I understand what Greta is saying. She is trying to show us that we are wrong to fight.'

'Brown Mouse Riverbank,' Snowy replied. 'I too believe this is what the human child says. For many years we have been at war for no reason beyond a difference of how we make our beds.'

'Now is not the time to place blame, but we Brown mice believe that it was the White mice that attacked us first and mocked us for our leafy beds. But we are not free from guilt. We fought and argued back in a way that was harmful.'

'I agree that we acted in an aggressive manner for the pettiest of reasons. Perhaps it is now the time to recognize the dangerous mistakes of our past actions, and move forward as a united species of mice.'

'Move forward united,' echoed Riverbank. 'Greta has shown us that judging one another can cause nothing but grief. Our argument has destroyed this once green and pleasant land. But together, we can move on from this long and painful battle.'

'Then united we will be,' Snowy said. Tentatively, slowly and a little nervously, the two war leaders held out their front paws for the other to take.

As their paws touched, the armies surrounding them threw down their weapons in a unanimous display of peace and joy. They boldly walked across the battlefield to embrace the mice that an hour earlier had been their enemy. Friends forced apart by the vicious war met and hugged one another for the first time in five years. Mice that had never spoken to a mouse with different color fur kissed each other's cheeks. Greta clapped her hands in delight and smiled broadly as the now united land of mice held each other's hands and turned to bow to her. Kyrie purred with pride and happiness at the young girl's achievements.

'You see Greta,' she said, laughing. 'You are strong, you are brave! You have stopped one of the longest-running wars of the animal kingdom! You have achieved more in this one day than many warriors achieve in their lifetimes. And yet, a small while back, you told me you weren't brave enough for this adventure. But look at you now!'

Greta smiled back, happy to have succeeded in putting an end to a war that had caused nothing but sadness.

The parties and celebrations quickly spread across the Land of Mice, as news of the peace spread. The largest was held at the center of the country, as Snowy and Riverbank walked hand in hand into the palace that had stood empty for the five long years of the war. Now it was decided to be shared between the Brown and White mice. To celebrate the unification of the land, Snowy and Riverbank called for a huge banquet to honor their country's newest hero, Greta. A great feast was cooked of dandelion and daisy stews, served with dew-drop wine. The two leaders raised their glasses to Greta and this new chapter in their history, with the promise that war would never again break out between the two tribes. Brown and White mice would live together in peace and harmony for evermore.

Greta's task in the Land of Mice had been achieved. But she

knew her adventure wasn't over yet. She still had to travel to the Rat Kingdom, and rescue Boris. The thought of what lay ahead still made her nervous.

'There really is no time to lose,' Kyrie said, yawning, as the two went to their assigned bedchambers in the newly re-opened mouse palace. 'The Rat Kingdom is the next land across from here. In fact, we're nearly there. But we've got to get past that tricky millpond on the border, and then get to the point where we can rescue the Prince.' She yawned again, lazily, as cats do. 'So we'd both better get some rest. Or else we'll be too tired to move on tomorrow!'

Greta nodded, resting back on her soft bed (made from a mattress of leaves). But one thing was troubling her. 'Kyrie,' she murmured, as she slowly closed her tired eyes. 'Kyrie, what's the tricky millpond?'

But Kyrie had already fallen asleep beside her, so Greta put the thought out of her mind, and went to sleep as well.

In which Greta faces the millpond

Kyrie and Greta woke that morning to see the sun streaming into their bedrooms – the first time the sun had shone on the Land of Mice since the war had begun. They could hear the mice running outside, joyous in their freedom from war and fear, able to enjoy the sunshine once more. Greta and Kyrie looked at one another and smiled, proud and happy with the work they had done here. They left their room and were warmly welcomed by Snowy and Riverbank, who, having spent the night and morning making each other's acquaintance, had discovered a mutual love of backgammon and chess. The four walked across to the palace's banquet room, where they were offered the largest selection of cheese and crackers Greta had ever seen. The table ached under the weight of platters of cheddar and Cheshire, red Leicester, three county, stilton, ricotta, mascarpone, camembert, feta, brie, gorgonzola, emmenthal, mozzarella…plus a feast of sheep, goat and cow cheese that Greta couldn't even name. After eating their fill (Kyrie had warned Greta to eat as much as possible as they might not be able to sit down to dinner for a while), the adventuring pair said goodbye to the mice, who thanked them over and over, and wished them luck with their mission; along with invites back to the palace should they ever pass through the Land of Mice again.

It was time to head to the border, and from there confront the Rat King.

'So, Kyrie, what is the millpond?' Greta asked, after they had been walking through the Land of Mice for a few miles. Now that the war was over, the landscape had begun to recover. Shoots of green were appearing from the dusty ground. They walked past groups of mice working together to rebuild their villages; Brown with White painting houses and halls in bright and merry colors.

'It is good you ask me that now, Greta,' Kyrie replied. 'For the border between this land and the Rat Kingdom is only a mile away, and that is where we'll find the millpond. So I suggest we stop here for some tea and maybe a snack or two from your pack, and I will explain. It is a dangerous part of our mission, so listen carefully.'

'The millpond is, as its name suggests, a pond of a mill. What makes these pools special is that they are almost completely still, giving a perfect reflection of anyone who looks into it. But beneath its peaceful exterior lies hidden dangers. The pond is endlessly deep and should you fall in you will be dragged down into its depths by the entangling weeds that grab and clutch at you as you fall in.

'What makes this millpond particularly unique is that not only does it give a reflection, but also it shows the viewer their true and inner self. If you do not believe in yourself, if you cannot face your true reflection as you look at it, then you will fall into the millpond. But if you have faith in yourself, then you will see your real face and will be safe.' She paused, to let her words sink in, before smiling softly. 'But you'll be fine, Greta. Think how much you have achieved so far. You surely believe in yourself by now. You just have to see how brave and good you are. You'll do just fine.'

Greta smiled weakly back, but she couldn't repress a shudder of fear. She didn't know if she was strong enough or brave enough to face the millpond. And she only had a mile before she must look into it! She gulped down the last of her tea.

'Come on Kyrie. We'd better keep going. We've got to get to the Rat Kingdom. We've got to get to Boris!'

Kyrie mewed in agreement as the two stood up to carry on with the journey. Greta could see that the closer they came to the border of the Rat Kingdom, the more desolate the Land of Mice became. There were no more villages, no more happy parties, just the thick woods looming ahead of them in the distance.

'Those woods mark the border,' murmured Kyrie. 'You can see

the mill from here.'

Greta's heart skipped a beat. Never had a mile gone so fast!

The millpond was beautiful. The old wooden mill turned slowly, looking like it had come straight out of a storybook. It was just as Greta had always imagined a mill would look. The pond itself was a deep shimmering blue, clearer than the summer sky, deeper than the petals of a forget-me-not – and yet it looked as cold and cruel as it did beautiful. Surrounding it were tall and elegant green rushes, tipped with white cotton or brown brushes. Behind it, the tall pines and oaks loomed menacingly.

'So here we are,' Kyrie said. 'Would you like me to go first?'

Greta shook her head. 'I don't think so. I think this is something I have to do. And if anything happened, then I'd be lost without you.'

Greta hadn't put that as well as she meant, but Kyrie appreciated the sentiment. 'Okay then, Greta. Just remember everything I told you. You are brave and kind and intelligent – you can achieve whatever you want. And you have done. Don't let anyone tell you otherwise. Never feel like you have to change to make people happy. You are who you are, and you should always, always be proud of that.'

Greta smiled uneasily and walked slowly to the edge of the millpond. The rushes brushed against her carelessly in the slight breeze that rippled the surface of the water.

'If you see any movement in the water, then think harder on believing in yourself,' Kyrie called, her voice a little broken. It wasn't that she didn't believe Greta could do it. She just wasn't sure if Greta knew that she could succeed.

Greta nodded back silently, and kneeled down at the steep edge. 'Here goes,' she said to herself. She concentrated hard. She thought about her beautiful bedroom where she always felt so at home, and about Boris, whom she always shared it with. She thought about the girls at school who were mean to her, but how she had refused to change to make them like her more, to fit in. She thought about how she had overcome all their nasty comments to get good marks at school, how she was smart and funny, could paint lovely pictures and write good stories. She thought about how no matter what people said to her or how bad they made her feel, she had never given in. She had stayed loyal to her views and opinions, even on the days when the only one who would listen to them was Boris. She thought about the future adventures she would go on to have one day. She looked back on what she had achieved in the last few days, her courage in standing up to the mice and in overcoming her fear on the staircase. She smiled at the thought of her eccentric parents, and finally she thought about the gorgeous blue-black cat she was here to rescue.

She looked down.

Looking up at her from the crystal glassy blue water was a face she recognized, and yet seemed strange to her. It was a smiling reflection, but beneath the merry eyes was a hard determination and strength that suggested a brave spirit that would not be subdued. It was a striking face, with green-grey eyes that were bright, intelligent and smiling. She could see in the face a fighting heart that wouldn't be placated or repressed. Greta shook her head, and the face shook back at her.

'But,' she said, 'but that's n...'

The water began to stir, and Greta became aware of the tangled mess of grasses and weeds moving under the still surface. The reflection looked back, a hint of fear in those brave eyes.

'Greta!' Kyrie miaowed. 'Don't stop now! Think who it is in the water!'

Greta stared and stared, trying to recognize the face that looked up at her from the water. She was frightened, yet deep down she knew she had the answer and that she just had to face it.

'But that is me!' she cried. 'Look Kyrie, see! That is me there! That is who I am. I am brave, and I am strong, I am all these things!'

Kyrie burst into peals of relieved laughter as the waters calmed and Greta stepped away from the pond. 'Of course it is silly! It's what I've been telling you from the start! You are all those things. You just had to learn if for yourself. Now do you believe me?'

Greta started to laugh too. 'Yes, yes I do,' she replied, hugging her close. 'I had no idea. But I am good. I can do this. I can do anything I want to, because I am all these brave and wonderful things. And no-one can change that unless I let them. And I'm not going to, Kyrie. I am not going to let anyone change me.'

'No, I don't think you ever will. Now, just let me look, and then we can be on our way.'

Greta let her go. 'Aren't you scared?' she asked.

'Oh no,' Kyrie replied. 'I know what I'll see.'

Greta smiled, as Kyrie looked over the edge, to see the reflection of herself that she loved and recognized; a peace-loving warrior who believed in the power of harmony. A heart that desired to heal division and help create better communities. A beautiful cat with an inner-strength that couldn't be stopped.

'Right then. Now we have completed the task of the millpond, we can cross that border and rescue the Prince!'

In which the border is crossed and they enter the Rat Kingdom

'Ok Greta,' Kyrie said, as they made their way from the millpond into the woods. 'There are some things we need to remember now that we have reached the Rat Kingdom. Never trust a rat. They will trick and they will lie to get what they want. Don't even trust the land you walk upon. Nothing here is as it seems, nothing is strictly safe. I've traveled to many lands and seen many wonders, but nothing scares me as much as the Rat Kingdom.'

Greta nodded in response, trying to put on a brave face. But inside she was terrified. For if Kyrie was afraid, well! That meant the Rat Kingdom really must be a terrifying place. Still, she reasoned, there was no turning back now. She took a deep breath, and steeled herself for the journey. She would just have to tell herself not to be frightened. After all, she had to rescue Boris!

The surroundings did not really fill her with much confidence. Unlike the sheltering trees way back at the start of their journey, this forest hung over them, dark and threatening. The branches were twisted and gnarled, the patterns in the bark making vicious faces that sent shivers down her spine. The birdsong that had begun to resurface in the Land of Mice had fallen silent. The only sound was the rustling of shadowy leaves and the occasional scurry that made Greta jump out of her skin.

'Kyrie,' she whispered. 'Have you thought of a plan to rescue Boris?'

Kyrie stopped next to a blackened old tree stump, and rubbed her side against it. 'I don't really know. I've been trying to formulate a strategy, but each one hits a dead end. I keep hoping that when we get there, the answer will just be obvious.'

Greta stood in silence for a while. 'Couldn't we just ask for Boris back? Ask the Rat King to do the right thing?'

Kyrie smiled. 'If only it were that simple.'

But maybe it could be that easy, Greta thought. Maybe it was the simplest plans that work out the best.

They continued their walk through the forest. It seemed to grow thicker and darker the further they went. And as they came ever closer to the Rat King's castle, Greta became more and more aware of red and yellow glowing eyes gleaming at them through the darkness. They were being watched.

'The rats have spies everywhere,' Kyrie muttered. 'There is no point hoping for an element of surprise in this place. Sometimes I think it's a shame that the Kingdom of Cats don't have more cats on guard, watching the land. Perhaps then Prince Boris would be safe at home.'

'But if the cats were so mistrustful and spying on everyone all the time,' Greta said, 'then the kingdom would not be as lovely a place to live as it is.'

'That's true. We cats do feel happy and secure in the kingdom because we have so much freedom.'

Greta agreed. She certainly didn't feel safe or happy here.

Kyrie nuzzled her head against Greta's knee. 'I may be frightened here, my friend, but you can be sure that as long as I am by your side, no harm will come to you. I would never let that happen.'

Greta leant her arm down and scratched Kyrie behind the ears. 'I know,' she said. 'And I will not be afraid with you by my side.'

The two friends looked at each other and smiled. Over the course of their adventure together, they had become close. Greta was sad that soon she and Kyrie would have to go their separate ways, as Kyrie would return to her travels and adventures. But for now at least, they were together.

'Come on then, Kyrie, let's keep going.'

As they carried on walking, the many red and yellow beady eyes followed their steps. Greta and Kyrie could hear the sinister, slithering sound of hissing and scuffling, as the rats started to surround them.

'Keep calm,' Kyrie whispered out of the side of her mouth. 'It looks like we are going to have to go along with them for a bit.'

Greta bit down on the side of her mouth and dug her nails into her palms. She was determined to not show any fear, as the largest rat she had ever seen stepped out of the shadows and walked towards them.

'By order of the Rat King,' he said, in a sniffling, high pitched voice, 'trespassers in this land discovered by spies and informers loyal to his great majestic self shall be taken immediately to the castle to seek audience with his Highness. He can then decide on the best course of action to punish any law breakers and trespassers who walk through this ratty land without due permissions or invitation.' He paused to recover his breath. 'Seize the intruders!'

At his word, the rats swarmed towards Greta and Kyrie, gripping their arms and legs with gnarled and clawed hands and feet. The pads on the rats' feet were rough and calloused; their nails were bent and crooked and dug painfully into Kyrie's fur and Greta's skin, pulling hair and whiskers. Greta felt deafened by the devastating cacophony of squeaks and squeals and threats. 'This is quite enough,' muttered Kyrie into Greta's ear. 'Just hold tight. I'm going to shout out.'

At that moment, Kyrie released from the pit of her belly a loud, caterwauling wailing MIAOW that silenced and stilled the squabbling, vicious rats. As they stopped, Kyrie held her head high.

'Thank you,' she said, shaking her smooth head as if to brush away the dirty touch of her enemies. 'I beg permission to speak, Envoy of the Rat King, and invoke the right of parlay.'

The Rat Envoy looked at her curiously. 'And how, may I ask, do you presume to know the right of parlay?'

Kyrie tossed her head proudly, determined to show that she

was not intimidated by this huge rat. 'The rats are a pirating species and parlay is the request to see the pirate captain on capture, without any harm coming to you in the intermediary period. As a mi-ke cat, my father served on pirate ships in both China and Japan, before he settled into his life as a fisher-cat. This means my family history gives me the same rights and protections as the pirates. Rats pirate on boats and on land, therefore I invoke the right of parlay. You and your followers will not touch or hurt myself or my companion until we have spoken to the Rat King and he has made a further decision.'

The Rat Envoy paused to consider the request. 'Your reasoning and argument is correct, cat. And according to the rules we cannot harm or touch you. If you would follow us to the Rat King, we will proceed from there.'

Kyrie bowed her head and gave Greta a satisfied grin. The two of them brushed themselves down, collected their belongings, and solemnly followed the Rat Envoy through the thickening forests, towards the castle and their meeting with the King. Greta could not think of a time she had been more terrified.

In which they meet the Rat King

The castle rose above them without warning. Unlike the grand beauty of the palace of the Kingdom of Cats, or the cheerful communities Greta had seen on her journey through the Milky Sea Port and the forests below the staircase, this castle seemed like something from a nightmare.

It was vast and sprawling, with twisted spires and turrets filthy with grey smoke stains, overgrown with hanging dead vines. Surrounding the walls was a filthy and polluted moat, from which rose a dank and stagnant smell. What could have been beautiful gardens were now unkempt and littered. The only surviving plants were greedy weeds, choking any life beneath them as they wrapped their coils around dead or dying shrubs and trees. The moon or sun was blacked out by billows of thick smoke rising from sputtering and choking fires that smelled of burnt rubber. Despite the flickering flames, the fires failed to warm the cold and damp atmosphere that filled the filthy air.

'Poor Boris,' murmured Greta, as she took in her surroundings. That her beautiful cat had been forced to live in such horrendous circumstances!

'If the King saw this,' Kyrie whispered. 'Our poor Prince!'

As the party walked into the castle's courtyard, Greta took a deep breath. The sight here was even more terrible than what she had seen outside of the castle walls. The scene was one of greed and cruelty. Rats lolled on their backs in gangs, swallowing from oversize goblets of beer and tearing at bones of meat, as their swollen bellies grumbled with painful indigestion. In other corners, deafening squeaks and shrieks were accompanied by punches and bites, as gangs fought each other for sport. The ground of the courtyard was littered with waste; discarded bones were nibbled on by cockroaches and other pests, whilst a tipsy group of bugs swam in a pool of spilt beer. The noise and the smells were overpowering, as Greta put her hand over her mouth to prevent the nausea rising in her stomach.

In the center of the chaos sat the Rat King, scarier, bigger and smellier than all his ratty subjects. He was sprawled out across his throne, flanked by two rats waving fans. In one scaly paw he held a goblet of ale; in the other he had a gnawed turkey leg. At the sight of the approaching party, he sat up abruptly.

'Ah ha!' he bellowed, his voice deeper and less slithering than that of his Envoy. 'You return with the trespassers! And yet, they look rather safe and calm.'

'Your majestical greatness,' sniffled the Envoy. 'The mi-ke cat invoked the right of parlay. Therefore, according to the rules, we could not touch them until they had spoken first to your excellent Highness.'

'Hmm,' he said, scratching his whiskers, which were wrinkled and uneven. 'So, the cat knows of the rules.'

'My father was a pirate cat before settling into a life of fishing, as was his father before him,' Kyrie said, her voice proud and haughty. 'Therefore you find the rules apply to my companion and me. We have come to speak with you.'

'Yes, yes,' he said, waving his gnarly old paw dismissively. 'I know why you have come. You have been sent by your King to rescue the Prince who my soldiers stole from you. But the question needs to be asked, why on earth do you think I would return him to you?'

Greta looked nervously down at Kyrie. Such direction was unexpected.

'Because it is your duty!' Kyrie cried out in anger. 'You have defied the laws and harmonies of nature! You have to restore order and do what is right!'

There was a brief pause before the whole crowd of rat courtiers exploded into hoots of laughter. They rolled on the floor, unable to catch their breath through the force of their hysterics. Tears of mirth rolled down the grubby cheeks of the

King, as gales and screeches of hilarity burst from his courtiers' bellies.

Kyrie stood there, her self-possession slipping away as she witnessed the dreadful reception her words had received. For one of the first times in her life, she was at a loss of what to do. Her training in the art of peace and war, her battles and travels, none of it had any meaning here in this land of greed and self-interest. These animals did not care about nature and harmony, they didn't care about the rules that governed the right way of life in the animal world. She looked up at Greta, who met her troubled eyes.

Greta understood. This was a challenge that she was going to have to face. If only she could think of a plan! The pair stood there as the laughter around them roared, looking desperately at each other, then to the King, and then back again.

'You foolish cat!' shouted the Rat King through his mirth, spluttering bits of gnawed food and chewed spittle out of his

mouth. 'Do you really think that I, King of the Rats, care about your foolish code of nature's laws! If I had done so, why, then I would not have captured your Prince to begin with. I am afraid you must think of a better reason than that.'

Greta stepped forward. She had to take a gamble. The longer she and Kyrie stood standing there, the more at risk they would be, and the greater the danger for Boris.

'You may not care about the code of nature,' she began. Her voice was shaky, but at the sound of it, the laughter stopped abruptly. 'And in that way, you are akin to my species, that of humans. But despite human ignorance and arrogance, we are still a species of honor. So, I ask you now, if we are also the same in that respect?'

The Rat King fixed her with his beady gaze. 'But of course girl-child. All creatures have a sense of honor. We rats are no different.'

Greta swallowed hard in an effort to stop her voice from shaking. She couldn't lose her nerve now. 'In that case, I take you on your honor and challenge you to a contest. Whoever wins will keep Boris.'

The Rat King looked around at his courtiers and smiled lazily. 'Girl-child, what contest could you possibly conceive of that would mean you would risk the safety of the Prince of Cats? What can you do that would make you so sure of your success?'

Kyrie stared wide-eyed at Greta as she made her pronouncement, her whiskers shaking. The rats moved forward greedily to hear how she would answer.

'I have only my sense of what is right to guide me,' she replied, her voice gaining in confidence. 'I know that my love for Boris makes me invincible against you. Therefore I have no fear in challenging you to a competition.'

'Strong words, girl-child, strong words indeed. But can you back them up, I wonder? What exactly is this challenge you have set your sights on?'

'You will swear on the honor of your throne to agree to and accept the challenge, whatever it may be?' she asked.

'Yes, girl-child, I do.'

'And you agree to the terms that whoever wins my challenge is allowed to keep Boris?'

'I do. Whoever wins the task will have the Prince of Cats. Just name your contest. I am the Rat King. I have traveled the world with pirates, I have kidnapped the Nutcracker Prince, just as I cat-napped your foolish Boris, and I have fought and won many wars. I have no fear.'

Greta took a deep breath. 'Okay. I challenge you to look in the millpond that reveals your true face.'

The crowd of rats that had been encroaching forward towards the pair collectively gasped, and took several steps backward. Kyrie put her head in one paw sorrowfully, but Greta kept up her steady gaze at the Rat King, awaiting his answer.

It was a long time coming. At her words, the King's first reaction was a look of horror, which he quickly suppressed and tried to replace with his previous expression of smug superiority. However, he had difficulty maintaining his air of confidence as he fidgeted with his paws and ran his shaking claws over his whiskers. He could not let his rat followers see it, but the prospect of this challenge terrified him.

'I accept,' he replied finally. 'I will keep my word. Whoever stands the test of looking in the millpond will win. If you can face your true self and avoid drowning, then you can take the Prince Boris back to the Kingdom of Cats. If not, he remains my prisoner.' He laughed a sinister sneer of a giggle. 'And I have a good mind to take you both as my prisoners as well!' He turned to his Envoy. 'Fetch the cat prisoner!' he ordered. 'And then we proceed to the border!'

In which the challenge takes place

It was a solemn procession that walked towards the border of the Rat Kingdom and the now united Land of Mice, where the millpond lay. Two rat soldiers led the way, followed by the Rat King on a sedan chair. He was flanked on either side by servants who carried a canopy to shade his ugly head.

Behind him was a line of soldiers, followed by Greta and Kyrie and the Envoy. Next walked another line of soldiers, and behind them came Boris and his prison guards. Greta was torn between sorrow at seeing her beloved cat being treated so badly and pride at his bravery. For Boris was not a cat to be cowed and afraid. Despite being in chains and led by the snarling and smirking rats, his noble head was held high and he maintained a stately pace, determined to show neither fear nor despair at his plight. He bore himself proudly, and despite the dirty dust and filth that covered the floor and walls of his prison cell, he made sure his coat was gleaming and glossy. His eyes sparked with defiance and disdain over the rat jailers.

Greta and Kyrie followed his example. Although terrified inside of the very real possibility of failure, Greta held her chin up and not a flicker of her inner turmoil showed on her face. She was resolute that the rats would not intimidate her – or at least they wouldn't see that they did.

Kyrie felt equally strong-minded. Despite a nervousness that maybe Greta had taken on more than she could handle with the challenge to the Rat King, she felt that any doubts on her part would only serve to make Greta feel afraid. And Kyrie did not believe that Greta could fail. She knew that she had to keep thinking of success, and pass on her positive thoughts to all around her. They had come this far together and the rescue of the Prince was in their reach. Greta had already faced the millpond and succeeded. Failure, as they say, was not an option.

You might think that because Greta had already faced the millpond and survived, then the task ahead of her was one of sure success. Unfortunately for Greta, it isn't that simple. In every situation where we are challenged in our self-belief, when we are afraid or when we think things may go wrong, then new obstacles arise that have to be overcome. Where we have succeeded once, we may become cocky and over-confident, leading us to fail a second time. Our selves change every day. Whereas before Greta had to look in the millpond to assert her identity and believe in her inner beauty and truth, she now had to believe in her bravery and ability to overcome terrifying obstacles, such as the threat of being taken prisoner by the Rat King.

As she walked behind the soldiers and ahead of Boris, closely flanked by the Envoy, Greta repeated a mantra over and over in her head. 'I can do anything,' she whispered under her breath. 'I can achieve whatever I want, because I am brave, because I am strong.'

'That's right,' Kyrie murmured to her. 'That is what you must cling onto, Greta. You can do anything, you are a good person. Your reflection will shine out full of life and promise, whilst the Rat King will see nothing but fear and hate.'

And what was the Rat King himself thinking? He gave out the impression of arrogance and strength, but if you looked closely, you would see his tail shaking from fear. For he had so much to lose in this challenge! He could lose his royal prisoner; he could lose the respect he commanded from his subjects. He could lose his throne. But even those struggles were not as great as his biggest fear of all. For deep down the Rat King had an idea of what he may see in his true reflection. And he knew that what he would see would destroy him, and lose him his kingdom. Although he had no principles or morals, he was no fool. He knew what he was and what it meant. He knew what lay beneath his cruel and tyrannous front. And the thought of it terrified him.

Of course, his subjects were oblivious to their King's inner fears. They had a great belief in their leader, one of the few beliefs they had, and trusted that he would have no problem winning silly challenges thought up by little girls. For sure, he had sailed on pirate ships, he had fought and won wars, he had kidnapped the Nutcracker Prince and had the audacity to steal the heir to the Cat Throne. He could not be frightened by some foolish child!

The woods and the castle were rushing away behind them and light was seeping in between the dark and threatening branches of the trees. Tufts of green grass were beginning to appear on the ground beneath their scurrying feet, although the flowers still retreated and hid their faces from the rats. As they got closer and closer to the millpond, a heavy silence weighed down upon the tense procession, as Boris, the Rat King, Greta and Kyrie felt fear and responsibility sit heavily on their shoulders.

'I can do this, I am brave,' Greta repeated over and over.

'Greta can achieve whatever she wants, if she just believes she can, oh please let her see that she can,' Kyrie said to herself.

'If I see my true reflection, I stand to lose everything,' muttered the Rat King. 'I could lose my entire kingdom, all of my glory! It cannot, it must not, be as I fear.'

'Greta has come this far,' thought Boris. 'She has overcome so much, and she loves me. That will save us all.'

Still, no matter how slowly they walked, how winding a route they took, how much they tried to convince themselves they had many more miles to go, the destination had to be reached some time. Eventually the path became lighter and there in front of the procession was the clearing in the trees where the millpond lay. Greta drew in her breath. How could something so beautiful be so full of danger! She thought of poisonous tree frogs, the terrible strength of gorgeous tigers, painful thorns on delicately fresh roses. Yes, she realized. Beauty and danger can so often go hand in hand.

The shout of the Envoy interrupted her musings.

'Here we all are, to face the challenge of the girl-child Greta in exchange for Boris, Prince of Cats. Whoever succeeds in facing the truth of the millpond will win the prize of the Prince. Should the girl-child fail, then her fate and that of her companion will be decided by the triumphant Rat King. There is no need to say what will happen if our King fails, as such an outcome is impossible. Hail the Rat King!'

'Hail the King!' rang the spitting squeaking reply of the rats.

'If you would step forward to address the King, girl-child,' said the Envoy, 'the contest will commence.'

Greta obeyed. 'How shall we play this?' she asked. She was determined to be polite. After all, she didn't want to anger the Rat King. And she had always been a firm believer in good manners. 'Shall we take it in turns, or shall we both look at the same time?'

'Same time,' replied the King abruptly. He himself was not one for courtesy, and his underlying fear made him even less civil than normal. 'That way we know straight away.'

'And if we both succeed?' Greta asked, voicing her second greatest worry.

'We'll see,' he sneered. 'Envoy! Count to three and we'll see our reflections on the third count.'

'Good luck,' Kyrie said.

'Hail the King!' the rats yelled out.

'One!'

'I can do this, I am brave, I am strong,' Greta muttered in her head. 'I can do this for Boris.'

'Two!'

'It won't do to lose all of this,' panicked the Rat King. 'It won't do at all.'

'Three!'

They both looked.

In the cool still waters that showed the inner truth of their souls, Greta saw a face. This time she had no doubts that it was her face looking back at her. She believed that she possessed those strong and resolute eyes, that the calmness born of courage was hers. Her love for Boris shone in her face, telling her that she was a success. She had saved him and nothing could frighten her again. She could take on anything and anyone because her belief in herself and her strength made her great and good. She smiled and the reflection laughed back at her, telling her she had survived the challenge. Kyrie jumped up and down and clapped her paws as Boris purred happily and loudly. She looked up. She had survived.

But the King! Such a happy fate was not for him! Gone was his vast size, his strength and cruelty, the steely glare in his eyes that struck terror into his enemies and enforced obedience from his subjects. Instead, he saw in the water a tiny and frightened rat, eyes wide with horror, shaking in fear. His true reflection revealed him as a coward, someone who hurt others out of fear and insecurity; a coward who bullies others to try and make himself feel good. The arrogant swagger hid a nervous skulk; the cruel glare was transformed into a frightened stare. His whiskers shriveled, his tail swished from side to side in fear, as the millpond began to stir and the weeds began to gather.

'NOOO!' he screamed, covering his eyes with his scaly paws

to hide his reflection from himself as he jumped back from the edge of the pool. 'I can't, I can't look, I can't bear it! It cannot be!'

The rats stood around him, open-mouthed and wide-eyed in horror. Their King! Too afraid to look at his reflection! And if it had made him so scared then what a terrible sight it must have been. He stood before them, shaking in fear. He was nothing but a coward defeated by some human girl, not the great ruler of their fearful kingdom.

'All bullies are cowards,' said Greta.

'Take your Prince, take your cat,' he yelled out, a sob catching in his voice. 'And get out of my land, get out of my kingdom!'

'Your Kingdom?' shouted the Envoy. 'Why, you have brought shame to the name of rat! You will have to fight to keep your throne from this day on.' He pounced to grab the crown from the King's head, as the disgraced King-no-more lashed out with his claws.

Kyrie looked at Greta, and then at Boris. 'I think we should get out of here, don't you? Before this fight gets out of control.'

Greta nodded, and hurried over to Boris to undo his chains. His guards had already abandoned their prisoner and rushed into the fray to try and get their greasy paws on the crown.

'Boris, I've missed you so much! I'm so glad you're safe!'

He nuzzled Greta warmly. 'My friend, Greta, you have been so brave! You took on the Rat King to save me. You have saved both my life, and the future of the Kingdom of Cats.'

'Your Highness,' bowed down Kyrie. 'I would encourage haste.'

'Indeed Kyrie. And thank you to you also. Your courage here excels all others once more. And you are right, let's get out of here! This isn't going to end well…'

At his words, the three brushed themselves down and walked quietly around the squabbling and screeching rats, as they fought to become the next Rat King. The crown was pushed around on the muddy ground, as the Envoy chased after it, greed for power shining in his eyes.

'Never learn will they?' said Greta, as the other two laughed in response.

In which they head back, together again

As they crossed the border into the Land of Mice, Greta felt full of love for all around her. Boris was safe and by her side, Kyrie had become her friend. The Land of Mice was looking rejuvenated and joyful and the traces of the war were fading fast. The rats had learnt that bullying and terrorizing others was cowardly, and she felt good and happy and strong in all she had achieved in the last few days. She kept looking down at Boris, his noble head and gleaming coat, his bright eyes full of love for his human and anticipation for his homecoming. Kyrie looked fit to burst with pride, constantly praising Greta and telling Boris about the adventures they had had together; what Greta had done and what Kyrie had done, who said this and who said that.

Leaving the woods that cast ugly shadows over the Rat Kingdom, they stepped into the sun that shone down on the land before them. The mice were out and about in their newly peaceful home. They waved and smiled warmly at the three travelers, offering them food and drink on their way. Everywhere they went, Greta was hailed as a hero of history and the adventuring three were offered the choicest cheeses and the tastiest snacks.

The three travelers called in at the united mice castle, where Snowy and Riverbank welcomed them with open paws – although they had to wait until they had finished another of their never-ending rounds of backgammon before attempting conversation. They were thrilled to hear of the defeat of the Rat King and the rescue of Boris, and once more Boris heard the narrative of how Greta's wisdom and bravery had put an end to their pointless and squabbling war.

Everywhere they went they were welcomed with smiles and laughter, which, after the dark days in the Rat Kingdom, made every town, village and home seem full of light and joy.

There was no smile larger though than that on Sam's wise old face as the warrior, the girl and the Prince approached his patient boat at the shores of the Milky Sea. He bounded towards them, hugging his granddaughter, nuzzling Greta and bowing down low to Boris.

'You did it, you did it! I knew you would!' he said, tears of joy shining in his eyes. 'You two girls, so good, I always knew, I could see from the start that you had success in your bones! But there is no time to lose. We must return your Highness to the Kingdom of Cats as soon as we can. As soon as we can!'

The three of them climbed into the old boat and set sail back to the Milky Sea Port, as they excitedly retold the story of their mission. Sam heard how Greta had stopped the war, faced the millpond, won Boris from the rats, and made it all the way back again. He laughed and nodded and congratulated, and soon enough they arrived at the port.

It was an emotional goodbye as they left Sam behind in his old wooden house, after a sit down and cups of tea and milk. Boris promised Sam rewards that he refused, saying that the honor of helping his Prince, Greta and his granddaughter was reward enough. Kyrie hugged him over and over, tearfully promising to visit soon. Greta promised the same, although quite how she would ever find her way back here she didn't know.

With Sam left comfortably in his house, the three considered the best way to return home.

'How did you get here?' Boris said. 'Did you take the staircase?'

Kyrie and Greta nodded in reply. 'Is there another way home?' Greta asked. The thought of going down the staircase made her a little nervous to say the least.

Boris smiled lazily. 'Indeed there is! Let's shoot the works. Travel back in style.' He let out three sharp whistles, much to Greta's surprise. She had no idea that cats were able to whistle so well. But then, she hadn't known that cats could talk either until a few days ago. Or that there was a Rat King, or…well, so many things had happened that would have seemed impossible a week ago. Whistling cats was the least of it.

At the third whistle, Greta heard a great beating of wings above her head. She looked up, to see a huge and glorious golden eagle coming in to land. His feathers shone like polished bronze, his eyes blazed as orange as the evening sun and he looked as strong as a tiger or lion. He was, without a doubt, the most impressive and handsome bird that Greta had ever seen.

'Your Highness, Prince Marmaduke Nikolai Boris Blue,' his voice rung out clearly. 'I am at your service. And may I add that it is marvelous to see you safe and sound after your ordeal.'

'Thank you Gryphon,' Boris replied. 'I owe much to my companions here, the girl-child Greta and the warrior Kyrie. But now we turn to you and request a ride back to my kingdom, to be reunited with my family and my home.'

'But of course, your Highness,' Gryphon replied. 'It would give me great pleasure and it will be an honor to perform this humble service. Just get on my back, and off we go!'

The three followed his instructions and with a great flapping of wings they flew off. For Greta, it was one of the most exhilarating times of her life. The rush of the cool wind against her face, the gentle and calming swish of the beating wings, the tranquil beauty of Cloud-Top Land and then the forest beneath them; all of it seemed magical as Gryphon sped them back to the Kingdom of Cats. He surfed on thermals and raced other birds, pointing out landmarks and historical sites, until they landed safely and wished him goodbye.

Boris and Kyrie were home.

In which we celebrate!

As they walked from Gryphon's landing point towards the palace, the entire Kingdom of Cats rushed out to meet them. Music was played on the streets as cats mewed out their thanks for Boris' safe return, their happiness at restored order, their love and respect for Greta and Kyrie. Bands played a processional march, and everyone danced and cheered to see the three returning safely. But all this excitement was nothing compared to what awaited them at the palace.

The throne room was full of decorations, flowers, streamers and balloons. Huge pictures of Greta and Kyrie adorned the walls. A massive banquet was laid out, with platters of fish and poultry – as well as a selection of luscious creamy desserts, from ice cream to tiramisu to panna cotta. Flowers covered the table and all around the great hall stood minstrels playing mandolins and wind instruments. The room was transformed to a scene of merriment and joy.

At the head of the hall, resplendent on their thrones, sat the King and Queen and their younger children, where they had been anxiously waiting for news of Boris' safe return. When the door opened to reveal him standing there, safe and home again, his overjoyed family ran across the room to take him in their arms.

It was an emotional reunion as they cried and laughed and cried some more, holding their oldest son and brother close to them, never wanting to let him go again. Then more hugs and tears for Kyrie and Greta, as the joyful family thanked and praised them; naming them heroes of the land and demanding that they take their place in the history books.

After they had hugged and cried and hugged some more, King Whiskers decided order had to be restored. He took his place at the head of the banqueting table and motioned for the rest of the court to do the same. Once everyone was seated it was time for his speech. King Whiskers was, after all, very fond of speeches.

'My dear wife, my beloved children, friends and citizens of this great Kingdom,' he said to the great cheering crowd in the hall. 'What a day this is! What a glorious victory! We have moved from the darkest times to stand united today in this bright and happy moment. The cat-napping by our enemies the rats of my eldest born son, Prince Marmaduke Nikolai Boris Blue, threw our land into terror and confusion. Sorrow gripped us and we did not know if he would ever be seen in our kingdom again. We did not know if the rats would win this round. Uncertainty took over and we sank into a national depression.

'But cats will never be defeated! By working together with our friends and loved ones we can achieve anything! This was the lesson learnt by the brave girl-child Greta. She overcame obstacles and terrifying ordeals to rescue our beloved Prince. Her courage and determination to succeed has brought back to us the good and noble Marmaduke Nikolai Boris. She has restored safety and harmony to our kingdom!

'But she did not do this alone. Our gratitude also extends to the legendary warrior, Kyrie. Never have we known a cat of her strength, her wisdom and her bravery. Without these two great women, our Prince may have been lost. So I ask you to raise a toast to my son's safe return, and to those who made it happen, Greta, Kyrie and Boris!'

Every cat in the room cheered and raised their glasses of dandelion wine in a toast to the heroes.

'You know me well,' continued the King. 'You know how I like to talk and make speeches and talk some more. But for the rest of the evening I will remain quiet. Let the warriors tell their story and let the celebrations begin!'

And begin they did! The minstrels struck up their songs, as the cats and Greta started to tuck into their food. The cats clamored around the heroic pair, begging to hear the stories of how Kyrie found Greta, and how Boris was rescued. Everyone was laughing and talking and laughing again. After eating their fill of the delicious meal the cats took to the dance floor, whirling around the great hall with elation.

Greta was happy too, but she felt strangely subdued – something that did not go unnoticed by Boris and Kyrie. After dancing together many times the pair came over and sat down next to her.

'Are you ok, Greta?' Boris asked, nuzzling his human's chin.

Greta smiled at the familiar caress. 'Yes, of course. It's a marvelous party Boris.'

'You just seem slightly sad,' Kyrie said. 'Not as lively as the rest of us. Are you sure there is nothing wrong?'

Greta looked sadly at her hands. 'I guess it's the opposite. I feel so happy here, with you both, and in the Kingdom of Cats. Everyone has been so good and kind to me. I feel like I don't really want to go home.'

Boris and Kyrie exchanged knowing glances.

'It is very easy to think like that Greta,' Boris replied. 'Sometimes, when you are so happy in a place, you can't bear the thought of leaving it. Especially if leaving it means returning to somewhere that can be not so nice. But the human world is where you belong. It is part of who you are. Just as here is where we cats belong. Think what would happen if you stayed here. You might be happy now, but you'd miss your family and your home and you'd lose a sense of your identity. You'd stop feeling human, you'd stop being Greta. And that would be a tragedy.'

Greta nodded. 'I suppose so,' she said. 'I just love it here so much.'

'Think of all that you learnt on our journey, Greta,' Kyrie carried on from Boris. 'What did you see in the millpond? A strong and brave girl who will become a strong and brave woman. You can take that with you forever now and you don't ever have to be afraid anymore. You've learnt to be proud of who you are, and that is such a great thing. Once you know that, you can achieve everything you've ever wanted and be happy wherever you go. You belong with your human world.'

'But you know you can visit here whenever you need or want,' Boris added.

Greta sat in a contemplative silence for a while. 'No, you're right. I see that. I cannot leave my place in the human world, or desert my family and my home. They are part of who I am. I should go back.' She looked at both the cats on either side of her. 'I'm sorry I can't stay for the rest of the party, Boris. But if I don't go back now...'

'Of course.' He nuzzled her happily. 'Do you know your way back?'

'I'll take her,' Kyrie said. 'Then I'll come back to the party.'

'Thank you, Kyrie. I'll see you tomorrow Greta, in my usual place! Thank you so much for what you did. Without you there to save me I dread to think what could have happened.'

Greta just smiled in reply, and Boris understood. They didn't need words.

Kyrie and Greta walked silently through the Kingdom of Cats to the border where it met the human world. Across the kingdom the parties and revels continued, but the pair felt sad. It was going to be hard to say goodbye to each other.

'You will come and visit, won't you, Greta?' Kyrie mewed.

'Of course I will! And you promise to visit me too?'

Kyrie nodded. 'I have so much respect for you, Greta. You have done so well and been so strong. Never doubt that. I am honored to have spent this journey with you.'

'I am too,' she replied. 'Yes. I am too.'

They smiled warmly at each other. 'Well, here I am,' Greta said. 'Time to say goodbye.'

Kyrie nuzzled her and the pair hugged for a long time. Then, with a final wave and without looking back, Greta returned home.

Epilogue

The sun streamed through the curtains, illuminating Greta's bedroom with dappled light. Slowly forcing her eyes open, Greta yawned lazily and stretched, trying to decide whether to sleep some more, or start the day. The sun convinced her to do the latter. She leaned over the end of the bed, and ruffled the top of Boris' head.

'Come on, time to wake up, Boris!' she yawned.

'Miaow,' he replied, yawning to reveal his rough pink tongue and shiny teeth. Greta dragged her tired body out of bed and wandered into the kitchen, Boris close at her heels. She put the kettle on, poured some milk out for her cat, made some toast with honey and together they went into the garden to enjoy their breakfast under the tree.

They had the whole summer ahead of them.

Acknowledgements

First of all I would like to thank the team at Our Street and John Hunt publishing who took a chance on Greta and Boris' adventure and chose to publish it. Thank you to John Hunt, Catherine Harris, Mary Flatt, Nick Welch, Stuart Davies and Trevor Greenfield.

Secondly I want to thank Robert Griggs for bringing 'Greta and Boris: a daring rescue' to life with his fantastic illustrations. They are exactly how I imagined the world of Greta and Boris to look. He is so talented and I am so proud to call him both a colleague and a friend.

Thank you to Bidisha for believing in Greta and Boris, and to everyone else who read the book and made me believe that it was good and worth publishing.

Thanks to Dave Sturdy for taking the 'author photo'.

Thank you to mum, Kathryn, Ben, Dad and Louise. To my friends, Liz, Liam, Emma, Cat, Coz, Mark, Tony, Chris, Duffy, Eva, Hannah, Nicky, Pip, Karen, Morvan, Julien and Natalie. To old friends Jay, Kay, Niz, Ralph, Holly, Joe, Lawrence, Nadia and Carol. And to London friends Dara, Doug, Dave, Kate, Rowan, Joe, Anna, Lydia, Ellie and Jack. Special thanks to Susie for collaborating with me on my other book The Light Bulb Moment and on the Crooked Rib Zines. Thanks also to my Bristol Feminist Network sisterhood, Anna, Katy, Sue, Jenny, Kate, Marina S and Helen, and to the feminist collective of tweeters for their endless encouragement and support.

Final and most important thank you to JP, who always believed in Greta and Boris, and in me as a writer.

OUR STREET BOOKS

Our Street Books for children of all ages, deliver a potent mix of fantastic, rip-roaring adventure and fantasy stories to excite the imagination; spiritual fiction to help the mind and the heart grow; humorous stories to make the funny bone grow; historical tales to evolve interest; and all manner of subjects that stretch imagination, grab attention, inform, inspire and keep the pages turning. Our subjects include Non-fiction and Fiction, Fantasy and Science Fiction, Religious, Spiritual, Historical, Adventure, Social Issues, Humour, Folk Tales and more.